Deep in the Wealden forest lies the old manor house, Mantlemass, the one constant factor in an ever-changing world. The Mantlemass novels trace the shifting fortunes of a family through two turbulent centuries showing how the lives of ordinary folk are touched by great events.

A Flight of Swans tells of Humphrey and Roger Jolland who are sent to Mantlemass after their mother's death to be cared for by their cousin Ursula Medley. The year is 1588 and the British Fleet is confronting the Spanish Armada. Excited at the prospect of a real adventure, Humphrey slips away to watch the great battle, and vanishes without trace. Roger, a frail child with a strange gift for knowing the future, is convinced that his brother is still living and will one day return.

Humphrey's disappearance brings his father Sir Francis Jolland to Mantlemass to search for his son. From the first moment, Ursula sees qualities in Sir Francis that she knows her own husband lacks. Roger is a bond between them.

Roger grows up at Mantlemass and becomes a part of the Medley family and, eventually, Master of their iron working at Plashets. But one day Humphrey returns. Roger's happy life is threatened by outside forces and he finds he has to make a difficult choice between his loyalty to his family and his loyalty to his men.

Other Mantlemass novels published by Macdonald

The Lark and the Laurel
The Sprig of Broom
The Eldest Son
A Cold Wind Blowing
The Iron Lily

Forthcoming titles

Harrow and Harvest
The Keys of Mantlemass
The Miller's Boy

A Flight of Swans

BARBARA WILLARD

Macdonald

Illustrations by Alan Marks
Cover design by Jerry Watkiss
Book design by Ewing Paddock

A Macdonald Book

First published in Great Britain in 1980 by Longman Group Ltd

This edition published in Great Britain in 1988 by
Macdonald & Co (Publishers) Ltd
London & Sydney

British Library Cataloguing in Publication Data
Willard, Barbara
A flight of swans.
I. Title II. Series
823'.914[J]

ISBN 0-356-13176-9
ISBN 0-356-13177-7 Pbk

Typeset by Leaper & Gard Ltd, Bristol, England
Printed and bound in Great Britain by The Guernsey Press

Macdonald & Co (Publishers) Ltd
Greater London House
Hampstead Road
London NW1 7QX

A member of Maxwell Pergamon Publishing Corporation plc

CONTENTS

1

'The Spanish are come!'

Exhausted as he was by the strenuous ride from London, Humfrey Jolland slept very little. Across on the far side of the stable loft, almost buried in straw, Robin Medley, who had the boy in his care, breathed so quiet and steady he could hardly be heard and might almost have died. The hot, comfortable smell of horses rose familiarly up the ladder and through the trap into the loft – familiar, truly, but not usually so near as to invade Humfrey's sleeping hours. He shoved at the harsh straw which, in spite of being covered by the cloak Robin had tossed him, still found ways to pierce the cloth and claw at his face. Humfrey's fifteen years had been spent richly – about the court, in great houses – and what would his father say if he saw him now, bedded in straw in the stable loft of a filthy inn? It came of being entrusted by his grandmother to her oafish country kinsmen of Mantlemass and Ghylls Hatch.

Not only physical discomfort kept Humfrey wakeful – he was altogether possessed by a wild excitement, a heady anticipation, by both fear and a puffed-up assurance of courage which was bound to drive him past common sense. For days and nights his ears had rung with that first cry of the rider who had overtaken them as they rode to London all those days ago to trade horses from Ghylls Hatch:

'News! News! The beacons are fired! The Spanish are come! They're come at last, sirs! Sighted off Portland!'

At this, it might have been expected, they were bound to turn swiftly, abandoning the London trade and the horses they brought to it, heading back without question or delay for Ghylls Hatch and Mantlemass where, at this time, Humfrey Jolland was a guest, and where his younger brother had been left behind with the women.

But Master Piers Medley, intent on his trading, and doubtless too accustomed to such rumours to give this one the attention it seemed to merit, had refused to turn.

'A fellow riding this road and nabbling of Portland can only be a man of hearsay.'

And however the others might argue and doubt and grumble and mutter, he stuck to his point. Only days later, most of the horses disposed of, and with London buzzing and humming with news of the great advancing fleet, had Master Piers changed his mind. The urgency of the matter could no longer be ignored. He was concerned at last to know that all was well at Mantlemass and Ghylls Hatch. He sent Robin off home with Humfrey, and would follow himself when the last beast was disposed of.

But by then Humfrey had plans of his own. They did not include returning tamely to continue as a guest of his countrified cousins at Mantlemass.

There was a sound below. Someone was crossing the yard towards the stable. Humfrey sat up in the straw, troubled lest its rustling should wake Robin. He must have slept himself more than he had supposed, for the faint light of very early morning showed him an outline or two. As he sat there, summoning his courage for the next move, his heart unpleasantly thumping, a cock crew far away and the first blackbird sounded sleepily among the laden trees in the orchard behind the inn.

The horses stamped and stirred below, blowing softly – and then almost immediately one of them gave a faint whinny. A man – no, two men, talking softly – came into the stable. A light showed Humfrey the square of the open trap, swinging, then steadying as the lantern was hung. The pair who had entered spoke in quiet voices that befitted the hour, yet somehow gave an impression of secrecy, of urgency. Straw rustled underfoot as they moved to their horses; leather creaked; metal jingled. They were preparing to saddle up.

Humfrey wormed his way cautiously across the floor and lay peering down through the trap, straining to hear what was being said. *The coast* ... quite certainly something about *the coast* ... Humfrey almost fell down the ladder in his eagerness.

'The ostler says we'd have done better to ride by Horsham,' one man said.

'They were all drunk. What good's a sot's advice?'

'Well – we're halfway to the coast by now, whichever the road.' His horse stamped, and tossed against the bit. 'Easy now. Be still, you damned brute,' he said, but softly and lovingly.

'Only let 'em dally till we come!' cried the second man, laughing. 'That's all I pray for.'

'Amen to that – for as I see it, once they're into the Straits there's little hope of a good showing. They might battle all day and we'd do no better than hear their guns!'

Humfrey was shaking with excitement. This was such good fortune he could hardly contain himself in silence.

Here were two of those very gentry he and Robin Medley had seen riding out of London in their tens and scores, intent only on getting to the coast and from some imagined point watching the great men o' war beating up-channel, with Howard and Drake and Hawkins pressing on their heels. Few of them had any great notion of the width of the waters, and some of them innocently supposed they might take a pot at the enemy on their own account ... From the first sight of them, Humfrey had had only one thing in mind – to give Robin the slip and join these hopeful travellers.

Now here was opportunity actually within sight.

The two in the stable below were young and well-dressed – acceptable gallants not sly adventurers. Humfrey let himself down a few rungs of the ladder. Immediately, the taller of the two looked up and called out.

'So there's a lad or two still living in this forsaken hovel! Give a hand here, boy – the landlord's as drunk as all the rest or we'd have had him out of his bed.'

Humfrey replied coldly, 'I am a traveller, sir, as you are.' He let himself down the remaining rungs and stood as haughtily as he knew how – and he was, as his cousin Ursula Medley, Robin's wife, had said, 'a stomachy lad'.

The young man grimaced and then laughed. 'I do beg your pardon, my dear good young gentleman. For all that – pray pocket your dignity and give a hand!'

Humfrey held the horse's head, while its master saw to the girths.

'Do you ride to the coast, sirs? Do you ride to see the Spanish ships?'

'Aye – to see them burn! And every damned Catholic sailor in them!'

Above in the loft there was no slightest stir. For certain, Robin still slept. It was a moment for quick decision and

Humfrey made his own without hesitation.

'I'd be glad to ride with you.'

The two young men laughed, one merry, one scornful.

'I've my own horse,' Humfrey said, jerking his head towards the next stall. In fact he had ridden Piers Medley's big Agon from London to here, since Piers had bought a delicate chestnut mare he wished to ride himself. 'I am bound for the coast in any case,' the boy said, losing no dignity, sounding cool and confident, 'but for certain I could do with company.'

'Ah, yes,' said the shorter of the pair, 'but I know your sort. You've run from home to see the fun – and who'll come after you? Some angry father cracking a great whip. We'd be at the end of the lash if he found you with us!'

'Let me ride with you! My fellow traveller in the loft reaches his home in a few miles more.' He looked from one to the other, but neither seemed over-joyful. 'I'll go alone if I must,' Humfrey persisted, speaking low, increasingly fearful that Robin was bound to wake soon, 'but travellers are best in company.'

At that the taller, more friendly man, shrugged.

'Well – maybe we cannot stop you if you ride close behind.'

'But we'll by no means wait for you if you fall back,' said the other.

Humfrey saw that they were all but ready to ride and he sprang to saddle his own horse. They would almost certainly tease him by hurrying, but there was only the one road to follow. He would catch them up very quickly on tall Agon, might even tease in his turn by overtaking them.

Now he was sure he heard Robin stirring. Then he realized his jerkin and cap were up in the loft, and for sheer good sense he would not ride out in his shirt. He began to fumble with the leathers and their buckles, and sure enough Robin called out, but very sleepily.

Humfrey went halfway up the ladder, reaching out for his clothes, saying at the same time,

'Get back to sleep.'

'What's afoot?'

'Horses restive. Go to sleep. It'll be light soon enough.'

Robin gave a great yawning sigh and slid back into silence. Humfrey spared no thought for the distress and anxiety he must feel when he awoke fully and found himself alone – though this was less from malice than from sheer inexperience and young arrogance. It was true that he was inclined to despise Robin, a Medley only by adoption and even more countrified and strange than the rest of them – but he did not think of that now. His heart was thumping so heavily that it half deafened him, he felt light-headed with excitement and the delight of his own resource and cunning.

A full three minutes after the two travellers had departed, Humfrey led out his horse, expecting with every second to hear Robin's voice again, but this time fully roused – waiting for a hand to fall on his shoulder, to snatch at the bridle ...

Nothing hindered him. He was across the yard and out into the road. The animal being so tall, he was obliged to use the mounting block, and again was delayed. Then at last he was into the saddle, disposing himself with a slight groan as yesterday's tender spots took the hardness of the seat. He gritted his teeth, kicked up the big horse – and was away.

Piers Medley's Agon had a raking stride and he went at the road as if he had been stamping at pasture for months. His restlessness side-stepped and started. Humfrey had all his time and attention taken up with the business of

staying on. Coming up a long ride he saw his two fellow travellers well ahead. At this rate he would soon be level with them, and as things were he knew he had little hope of falling into an orderly cavalcade. But now the sky had lightened so speedily that the need for company had left him. He could manage very well alone.

Ghylls Hatch lay on Humfrey's left, with Mantlemass a few miles further east. At Ghylls Hatch, in the care of Ursula, Robin's wife, Humfrey's young brother awaited his return. These kinsmen had seemed all that the younger boy needed, but Humfrey found them so plain in their ways he could barely credit the relationship. Yet at Mantlemass his grandmother had been born a Mallory, and had married back into the Jolland family from which her own grandmother had come ... On that side even Humfrey had to accept the age and dignity of the family. But the last Mallory was long gone, there were only Medleys now. How little they regarded themselves was clear in the way they ignored their inheritance. No coat of arms was displayed, and even the great ring Master Piers always wore, though it carried an engraved emblem, seemed only a memento of the past. 'My father's ring.' Piers had said once. 'My father's and my grandfather's ...'

Within the next few minutes, Humfrey had caught up with his two riders and passed them with a shout. Two miles on and he and Agon were locked in a battle of wits and sheer physical strength. They had come to the crossing of the forest and the horse smelled his home.

Humfrey was a competent rider, but he had never before been called on for so much skill and cunning. Over the weeks of his reluctant stay at Mantlemass, his cousin Richard Medley had constantly dropped hints about his horsemanship – 'Neither sad nor splendid,' he had called it; but without scorn. And that was unlike his older brother – for Piers Medley had shouted and turned pale when he noticed Humfrey sawing at his horse's mouth. However unwillingly, Humfrey had picked up a lot of good sense from these despised countrymen, and Master Medley had acknowledged as much by putting him up on Agon.

Now his own prowess filled Humfrey with exaltation and he did not care that he had lost his cap, that the wind tore through his hair and his bared teeth, that his supposed travelling companions would never be seen again. His horse had wings and so had he.

Now the sun swam up on the summer day – the sky like fine porcelain, the trees heavy, the last dog-rose faded, the fields well coloured for harvest. The forest was left behind, the battle was over, horse and rider moved and thought as one, and neither tired. Soon the downs were ahead, swelling against the distance. Even by the time their summit was reached, the day still grew in splendour, second by second. Humfrey reined in at last and listened. The air mysteriously throbbed, yet he knew he heard nothing, the beating was within his own head.

He ran his hand down Agon's satin, sweating neck and the horse shivered, tossed his head and was ready to be off at once under a sun already hot and promising to shine without abatement until this new day's end. Ahead lay the sparkling ocean, blissful and serene, offering at this distance nothing more alarming than a few bobbing fishing boats.

Yet somewhere this side of the horizon, the Spanish ships were breasting up the channel under full sail . . .

It was Friday, the twenty-sixth of July. The year, which was the sixteenth of Humfrey Jolland's life, and the most important, was also the thirtieth of the Queen's reign; the year 1588.

'Get on, then,' Humfrey said to Agon; and they began the descent down the fair sloping sides of the downs.

Humfrey had not been to this coast before, though he had once been taken to see his father embark at Dover for a mission in France. He came now to a small sea-port, little more in ordinary times than a fishing village, but today noisy with expectation. Men bustled and ran, shouting to one another as they went. They had a little cannon mounted on the jetty and with it were prepared to take on the might of Spain. The harbour was full of small boats and these were being loaded – mostly with provisions, but some seemed also to be taking aboard men with weapons and with ammunition. It was the movement of pygmies against a horde of giants, but Humfrey's manly sophistication deserted him. His spirits rose to the scene, full as it was of courage and high anticipation.

Up from the shore, a dubious looking inn and a couple of dirty ale-houses supplied the needs of the little port. To fulfil his purpose, Humfrey needed a good lodging for Agon, feeling a great deal more responsibility to him than to Robin Medley – who would have woken long ago to anger and anxiety.

He rode on a little, supposing he must continue along the coast to the next haven. But then he saw another and more decent inn, standing back, with some good stabling. It bore the arms of a noble family, lords of much land in these parts. In its yard there was as great a bustle as below on the shore. Hams and huge joints, casks of wine and ale and great skeps full of fresh baked bread and mounds of green vegetables were being stowed in carts. The landlord himself, by the looks of him, was ordering the business, urging on his men to speed and effort.

'That's one load for the *Mary Bess*, and one for Ben's *Seabird*,' Humfrey heard him shouting. 'And that's all to be mustered this day. And say to his lordship, it's my best provender and welcome to it. And, God willing, we'll find more to'morrer, come there's need.'

His wife stood by the door, her hand to her mouth, watching all the good stuff ready to be carted away.

'There's never a penny piece'll be seen back – and all the ham gone – and all the salted pork. A starveling winter to come for every soul in this place!'

'Is it for the boats, goody?' Humfrey asked, dismounted now and leading Agon.

'Oh, aye – for the boats, surelye. The fly-boats come all along the south shore, sent by Lord Howard – calling out for supplies else the sailors starve. They bin all but a week on the tail o' the Spaniard, and their victuals is ate up, poor souls.'

'Has there been a great battle?'

'Naun that was heard here, sir. They say there was a flurry further west – Portsmouth, or some such. But there's no shot fired that I heard.' She clapped her hands to her cheeks. 'What if there's niver no battle, and bread and ale and meat all gone for nothing!'

'No battle?' cried Humfrey. 'How should there be no battle? Our enemies are at hand and threaten us.'

He spoke so loudly and heroically that the landlord looked round and then came towards him, eyeing Agon as he did so, and walking round him once before speaking.

'That's a fair nag you have there, sir,' he said. He gave a great wide smile. 'Shall I wager its breeding?'

'Why – if you must,' Humfrey said, uneasily. Surely he could not be looked for already? Could any animal living have made the journey faster than Agon?

'That come from Medley o' Ghylls Hatch, so I'd say.'

'Truly so. And needs your stabling, landlord.' He thought he caught a gleam of doubt, even suspicion in the man's eye. Did he think the horse was stolen for a quick flight, or some childish escapade? He said quickly, 'The horse belongs to Master Piers Medley of Mantlemass. I have it from him. He is my kinsman.'

'Well, then, sir, I shall care for the beast like my own. My grandfather served Master Piers's own father – and my mother, too, could tell of Mantlemass. Where do you journey, sir? Shall you bait yourself? There's still bacon boiling and not all the ale's gone to sea. Though by the way the mistus huffs you might think so!'

'I'd sooner the ale and I went to sea together,' Humfrey said boldly.

At that the landlord gave a huge guffaw. 'So that's your business, is it? Well – not the only young gentleman to sail out, neither! A good seaman, are you? If so – well, we'll ask Ben. Ben'll take you for nothing more'n your company – and see you safe ashore agin. And I'll be sure your horse do well while you're away.'

It seemed so easy that at this point Humfrey almost took fright and withdrew altogether. But the landlord had moved back into the yard and was already calling to Ben that he had a passenger. And since Ben was anxious to get to the shore and see his boat well loaded, there was nothing, short of cowardly retreat, but to follow as boldly and swaggeringly as possible.

In the bright sun, on an easy tide, the fishing boat loaded with supplies set out with a crew of four and one passenger. There was no swell once they were over the gentle breaker. It was easy for Humfrey to feel with confidence that he was a good sailor. The men at first took no notice of him, busy about their sail. But when they were settled and moving steadily out to sea, Ben touched his forelock to the young gentleman, telling him they were bound for any English ship that loomed ahead of them.

'They'll give us a welcome, I reckon,' Ben said. 'Though the dear Lord knows if we'll see our money for it. There's some'd turn back again if no pay got handed over. But the landlord's a true Englishman and never would bargain at such a time. More fool he, so says his mistus!'

Though the distance was hazy the wind freshened as they moved out of the shelter of land, and they increased their sail. Then their speed increased, too, and it seemed to Humfrey that no moment in life could be grander than this – the sun, the sea, the obedient boat, the rough salty men. And above all the strange threatening of battle, death and destruction, all held under the smile of the fair weather.

'Sail a'starb'd!' the look-out shouted.

For all the sun and the glitter on the water, a faint gauze of mist hung between the yawl and the great man o' war suddenly rearing above them. The wind took her as they gazed, and her canvas swelled, resisting, then filling with a sound like gunfire. Her rigging sang. Above her and around her, a dipping, saluting, screaming escort, hundreds of seabirds wheeled and rose, wheeled and fell swooping to the water's face, and like some great bird of legend she breasted the water as gently, for all her height and bulk, as if she were a vision of herself.

'I never saw the like,' said Humfrey.

'Aye, she's a fair sight,' Ben answered him, grinning a little at his inexperience, yet glad to be the wiser man. 'And four hundred men, maybe, aboard her. And that taking no count o' the rowers . . . Look there!' he cried, his voice rising. 'It's the whole squadron, seems like!'

Humfrey saw then, behind the first ship like its shadow, a second ship; and then, the shadow of the shadow, another, and then still more, but fading into the haze. Suddenly all the sea and the sky ahead and around them was full of billow and movement, huge walls bearing against the wind. Like ants men swarmed, while somewhere in filth and darkness the rowers waited on their benches, not straining as they must when battle was joined, but resting, breathing deep while still they might, waiting in the gloom for the pitch and speed of conflict, the threat of abominable death.

'See there! See there!' a man behind Humfrey shouted. 'Ben! See there!'

But Ben was standing in the bow, hailing the leading ship, his voice coming surprisingly clear and strong from between his cupped hands, echoing against the hull and beating back to them.

'Ahoy, there! Ahoy! Supplies from shore! Ahoy, ahoy!'

There was a boat putting out to them already, and another lowering. Only as Ben's final brave *Ahoy*! rang out, the mist cleared like a curtain smoothly drawn.

Someone shouted,

'They're Spaniards!'

2

The Younger Brother

For many days and nights, even after the battle was done and won, the beacons smouldered on the hill tops, now dying to a quiet air, now flaring as a wind rose and breathed fresh life into embers all but exhausted. When a breeze blew at midnight, then the glow could be faintly seen at least on those eastern tops, the last to be lit as the message flared up and across from the west country. The tired red eyes still watched, as if danger could not be altogether past.

And there were many who said that the great ships, battered as they were, might rally and re-form and breast again towards the English shore. Others, more sanguine, or with better reports, knew that the battle was over, the Spanish ships in full retreat, many fine galleons battered or altogether disabled or burned and sunk deep, along with flat-bottomed carriers, their companies of invasion troops drowned and lost utterly. They had cut their anchors and fled before Drake's fireships; it seemed suitable that as fire had warned of the enemy's approach, so fire had brought about the end.

Of one thing every sort of opinion was assured – God in

his wisdom had made one Englishman the comfortable equal of a dozen Spaniards.

On the height above and beyond Mantlemass the beacon was now nothing but a heap of dead ash. Each day since it had been fired Ursula Medley and the younger Jolland brother had gone up the steep track to see how it fared, and had at last scattered the remaining embers. It was most particularly their beacon – the men folk being from home, they two alone had been by it when the message was flung at last from summit to summit.

'We did middling well by the task,' Ursula said for the twentieth time at least, and still sounding proud and pleased. 'You for the doing, cousin Roger, and me for the urging on!'

She laughed, but Roger Jolland did not respond. The sun shone over the forest as Ursula stood looking down on a world so familiar she barely saw it; knowing without seeing that a pair of hawks hovered languid overhead, that the heather was fading from purple, that the summer was all but done. She looked round for the boy, and saw him leaning over the ashes of the great fire, stirring them with a stick. *Our cousin is a shade otherly*, she had written in that great rambling book she kept for recording daily matters. She had not meant that he lacked any of his wits, but rather that he saw too much. *His eyes are open where ours are closed* . . . What precisely had she meant by that?

'What is it that you find there, cousin?' She was troubled that he seemed suddenly so withdrawn. There were those, it was said, who could read the message of past and future in smoke and fire and water – then, given that seeing eye she felt was his, why not in ashes? 'What are you about so deedily?' she cried.

He flung down the stick and turned away. Before it could be hidden she saw his face and began to tremble.

'My husband ...?' she asked, certain he must report disaster.

He shook his head, then shuddered and put his hands over his face.

'Master Piers, then? Or Master Richard?'

'No ... No ...' He mumbled something, then repeated it as she frowned. 'When shall they get home?'

'Master Piers and the rest?'

'Aye ...'

'Why, any day now – any hour, surelye!' Because he had asked a simple question she recovered with an effort, and to distract them both began chattering. That morning a traveller from the coast had paused at the door to tell the latest news, as such did, to gain a bite in payment. 'Did you hear what he told? So much wood along the tideline it might build a hundred barns! And bodies, too – drowned men heaped up.' But the chatter did not distract, and she said, attempting to seem casual, 'Why did you ask – when will they be home?'

He stood with his eyes closed, biting his lip, swaying slightly, and her patience suddenly snapped.

'Rouse up, you great ninny! It's dinner time past. I'll stand here no longer prating wi' a mumchance lad!'

She swung off, then checked a little; being, as she had said of herself, 'a shade stately' with her third child. As she went down the bankside, she recalled how Roger had told her, as surely as if he saw the babe already in its cradle, that she would have another son. She had believed him. She believed him still, and so might have to believe what else he could have to tell. Maybe it was because he was a frail boy, with a slight weakness in one leg, that he had been given instead a power of the mind that was above the ordinary? And though she knew that such powers often came from the devil, she could not believe the child

touched by anything ungodly.

She turned back and held out her hand. At once he ran to her and pressed against her, and she put her arms round him and held him, offering him warmth and comfort – poor soul, his mother was only two months dead – why else had his grandmother sent him and his brother into the country save for change and solace. It was cruel indeed to speak harshly to him.

'God forgive me!' she cried. 'And do you, also, Roger Jolland, forgive your poor kinswoman for speaking so huffy and hard.'

He shook his head, clutching at her childishly. He said something, but too low for her to hear.

'Speak louder, cousin.'

'I said . . . I said, my father has another son.'

'For sure he has. Your brother Humfrey – that bold lad I tease for his pride – that shall be Sir Humfrey one day.'

He shook his head. 'No – no; the other.'

'John?'

'Aye, John. Younger than me – but better made. He is the third son – nine years old . . . John shall be my father's heir . . .'

'Why, why? What are you saying? Now perk up, do. They'll all be home soon – my husband, and Master Piers, and his brother and your brother, and all the servants we've missed – all safe home!'

'Not my brother,' he said. 'Not mine. Not Humfrey. We'll not see my brother Humfrey again this long, long day . . .'

There were seldom guests at Mantlemass these days. The time had passed when a casual traveller was likely to beg a bed, though none would be refused. The countryside, even the forest itself, had opened. Vast quantities of wood had gone to fuel the furnaces smelting iron; there were more and wider tracks than there had been even three and four years ago. A local man might from time to time be asked his services as a guide, but on the whole the traffic was carried elsewhere. There were roads that bridged many of the boggiest places. These high roads were infamous for winter mud, summer ruts and dust, but even the single horseman was more inclined to travel them as being at least well marked.

So that in one way the growth of traffic on increasing roads across the countryside isolated Mantlemass and others of its kind, leaving them to the importance of their own concerns, turned in upon their own small communities and looking warily at strangers.

And these forest people had secrets to guard, for they plied a trade that was open to envy. The processes of forging and firing, the mastery of iron that had made the Wealden country prosper, were fiercely and sullenly protected. Yet some could falter in the face of high rewards, and in these deep remote places foreign spies and native traitors flourished as they had done since the beginnings of the industry. It had been said that when the Spanish came there would be Sussex guns firing from both sides . . .

The Spanish had come and they had gone, and who would ever tell if men had been slain by weapons forged by their brothers? Or if they could tell, what profit was in the knowledge? Death had the last word and God ordered all.

In the afternoon of that same day, Ursula was in the kitchen, with Agnes Goodale, who was the children's nurse, and the rest of the Ghylls Hatch maids. They were ringing apples, the early crop off two ancient trees that grew at Mantlemass. The apples were peeled and cored and sliced, then strung on rods to hang in the warm and dry. The women all sat around the heavy great table, that was bleached with years of scrubbing, scored by many a slicing and chopping. Under the table, among the assortment of feet and ankles and skirt hems, waiting for any casual titbit his mother or the others might see fit to drop, was young Simon, two years old, very quick to scuttle from one spot to another as he saw his advantage.

'Chase him away, cousin!' Ursula said to Roger, working hard to cheer him. And he did smile a little, but looking at her so deeply that she escaped into exasperation, and sent him brusquely to fetch her a sharper knife for the apples. She felt his dependence on her and returned his affection, but was anxious to see him more independent. He must, she thought, have been far closer to his mother than Humfrey had been, who did not or would not mourn.

The need to confide her worries was hardly to be endured. Should she speak to Agnes of the boy's strange behaviour, his seeming gift of mysterious sight. Agnes was far more than a servant, she was a trusted and loyal friend. All the same, she was a countrywoman, born into considerable superstition, and might draw back in horror – as if from sorcery, from devilment . . .

Ursula rose from the table before the task was finished. She untied her apron and gave it to Agnes, saying,

'I must speak with my mother.'

'Shall I go with you?'

'I'll go alone.'

'Do you watch out and step easy, then,' Agnes said. 'This is no time for a stumble.'

'Leave pestering,' said Ursula; she went at once from the kitchen.

The sun had withdrawn and left a dull heavy light, a

breathless air. The weather echoed her own mood, that had started easy and now was all fret and anxiety. She was glad to be alone with her worries, but she was barely free of Ghylls Hatch when she found Roger Jolland running beside her.

Ursula paused.

'Cousin,' she said, 'we have bin all this day side by side. Now I'm set off on matters of my own knowing. I need no company. Get you back. I'll be home before dark come.'

'But if any should return ... If they should ride in –?'

'Then I can wait another hour, and so must they for greeting.'

She turned away firmly, but then once more relenting she paused and looked back at him, pointing to the sky and calling,

'Look! Look! There go our swans!'

Against the dull sky the birds looked white as moonlight, alabaster against lead. She counted them as they went over – seven, and then as always the one that lagged behind. Often they went over twice a day, flying from the big ponds to the north-west down to the marshy ground along the far river, returning at evening, as they were returning now, to sleep by the quiet water.

'What did I tell you about them, cousin? Do you remember?'

'Aye. I remember,' he called back; and this time he smiled, so that she went on her way with a lighter heart.

Yet what she had told and what he remembered made her sigh as she walked the familiar track to her mother's house. 'They mate for life – as we do,' she had said. She was reminded of many things – most of all she thought how her girlhood was gone for ever, while ahead lay only the long slow woman's journey into her own painful wisdom ...

Ursula's mother, Lilias Godman, was walking in her garden. Two years ago the ore that supplied her furnace at Strives Minnis had failed; the ground was altogether worked out and had to be abandoned. Surprisingly, Lilias had washed her hands of the business. The men who had worked for her, happy to call her *Master*, moved to Richard Medley's foundry at Plashets. They took with them what had always belonged to Lilias and to Strives – her trade mark of the Iron Lily. It had become, with her blessing, the Plashets Lily, increasingly famed as Richard Medley prospered.

Now Lilias lived alone at Strives, with none but Nance Tester to care for her. Lilias cultivated her garden, growing herbs in profusion, distilling as she had learnt to when she was a girl, finding in her later years a different fame. That there was now an air of dereliction about Strives, the ponds invaded by iris and lily and tangling weed, seemed not to trouble Lilias.

Ursula called as she came down the last long bank towards the house. Lilias was bending to snatch at some weeds. She looked up, straightened herself and went to meet her daughter.

She said at once, though not in any flurry, since that was not her nature,

'What's amiss?'

'Naun I'm certain on.'

'What then? Sit down, girl. You traipse too far at this time. Did you never learn the lesson of losing your first?'

They went up to the house and sat together on the bench against the wall.

'Mother,' Ursula said, 'they are long from home. They are too long, seems me.'

'With that many horses to trade?' Lilias gave her a rather reluctant smile. 'You forget how things go. All the long years Master Piers took – all the care and disappointment and the long toil of it, building the Ghylls Hatch line again after the great trouble there … Then is he to scamble the business of seeing his fine beasts sold and settled?'

'The Spanish could've landed. Why'd they not come home?'

'The Spanish! There's more than Spain needed to hobble Master Piers Medley!'

Ursula smiled at that. It might be that her mother was wiser in the ways of Master Piers than any of them. She spoke softer of him than she spoke even of his brother Richard – she understood his temper and could always cheer him. 'Fetch your mother here to me, daughter Ursula,' he would cry when a black mood was on him. And Lilias would go to Mantlemass and argue and bully till he began to laugh.

'Well,' Ursula said, 'I'm all nett-up by young cousin Jolland – or I might speak more sense.' She hesitated, uncertain how Lilias might take what needed to be told. 'That child see what we cannot.'

Lilias did not reply at once, but looked at her daughter in a keen, considering way.

'It might be,' she said at last.

'Then you see it too?' Ursula cried. 'You see it as I do?'

'Such things may be.'

'But there's no sin in it! He's little more'n a baby, someways. And much put upon by his brother Humfrey. There's no love between them.'

'Aye – a bold, contrary lad. I see him overbear the younger – and that one's weak in more than a bit of lameness.'

'Not weak in his head, mother, that I do promise. And he's brave enough when he's pushed – you should've seen him that night we lit the beacon. But – he's truly meek in a strange way.'

'God's fool – that's what such are like to be called ... I've yet to learn what about him irk you so?'

'He said – this very morn he said it though I could not firstly tell if he spoke in sorrow or only fear – he said that his brother Humfrey shall not return here.'

'And why should he? They're in London, and there's his father's house, and it's easy seen he's no bent for country living. I see him despise us here, the grummut! For all he was sent here for solace since his mother died, he's found no benefit. Let him go, I say, and little sorrow.'

In spite of her heavy fears, Lilias's familiar blunt manner made Ursula laugh. And truly she spoke good sense. They had all been sore miffed by Humfrey's high ways and contemptuous manner. She knew that Master Piers had done everything possible to favour him – taking him down for riding faults, then honouring him for correcting them, letting him ride the prettiest filly when they set out for London, a three-year-old grey for whose sake they were to make a slow and careful journey. That Humfrey had considered the mount his obvious right had been all too clear. Nor had he pleased Ursula when, looking at the train gathered ready in the early morning, he had said with a laugh. 'So many? What'll be left at Ghylls Hatch once we've ridden this lot away?'

Because he had put his finger on one of her worries, Ursula had not been able to forget the incident. It had not needed her mother to remind her of the weary years between the destruction of Ghylls Hatch and its renewal. But she knew it was the poorest management to sell so soon and so many. Either Master Piers was beginning to lack judgement as he grew old, or else he had been persuaded by Robin, whose eye was for gain rather than good sense. Ursula could not decide which possibility was the less distressing.

The laugh that Lilias had conjured up for her changed itself to a sigh.

'I've a draught'll soothe you,' her mother said. 'Come inside and drink and you shall be the better of it. And let you forget about men who stay from home, and be busy with your own purpose. Cherish your children, in and out of the womb!'

Later, when it was all but dark, Lilias saddled up her old chestnut, Folly, stolid in her age, and walked her daughter home. The two went in silence. The forest spoke more than they as night-time creatures roused and snuffled, barked and whined, flew hooting on purring wings, or churred in the heavy warmth of the late summertime.

They came to Ghylls Hatch, and Lilias helped her daughter from the saddle. Mother and daughter rarely embraced, but now they were close. Lilias hesitated a second, then bent forward and kissed Ursula's cheek, pausing long enough to speak in her ear.

'God keep you,' she said, 'and what you carry.'

As if ashamed at such softness, she pushed Ursula away, but Ursula caught her hand and held it.

'Mother,' she said, 'leave that solitude you dwell in and go to Mantlemass. There's none to sprug up the place and keep the maids to-work. There's men alone in that place since Mistress Susannah died, go and care for 'em – you know how often Master Piers has asked it. I'll bring your grandchildren to visit every day.'

'What is it you lack, child?' Lilias asked, still in that low voice.

'Maybe I'm like the boy,' Ursula said. 'I lack my mother. Pray, then – think on it.'

Lilias did not reply. She pressed Ursula's hand and turned aside. She mounted easily and swung Folly's head. Without saying a last good night, she rode away and the darkening forest swallowed her.

Ursula stood biting her lip. She had all but confided other worries, had almost said, 'I am no longer a girl in love. Life has changed and so have I. So has my love Robin – alas too much. Marriage, after all, is not such a happy dream . . .'

This was a weapon for reproach she would be a fool to put into her mother's hand. Lilias had chosen a very different husband for her daughter and had certainly not forgotten.

A hot and misted moon was rising as Ursula turned to go indoors. The Ghylls Hatch they had re-built on the ruins of the old was simple and solid and she loved it as her home. Yet she moved towards it now with little feeling of homecoming. Truly Lilias's infusion of herbs had soothed for a time, but now she returned to the worry of young Jolland's strangeness and what it might foretell.

As she put her hand on the latch she realized there was more light within the house than she would have expected. At the very instant she opened the door, Agnes Goodale came running to her across the hall.

'Madam – they're come! They're home!'

'All . . .?'

Then seeing the woman's stricken face and how she hardly dared shake her head, Ursula went by her saying,

'It had to be.'

Hearing her voice, Piers Medley had come to the door of the parlour. He held out his hand, and she went to him instantly.

'I know what you have to tell,' she said.

3

'Your brother is lost . . .'

Ursula stepped into the parlour. Young Jolland was waiting there and she put her arm about him, ashamed that she had rebuffed him earlier. She looked sharply about the room, seeing her husband sprawled on the settle next the hearth and Master Richard Medley at the table, his head on his hand.

'Where is he?' she demanded. 'What come to Humfrey Jolland?'

'Pray for an answer to that, daughter,' Piers Medley said. He sat down in the great chair at the head of the table, for he was master here as in his own house, though they all knew that Robin should have assumed the place long ago. 'He has gone. He has been sought these many days. No sign come to us he's still alive. God help me, I am answerable to his father.'

'He's not dead, sir,' the boy said suddenly, his voice light and wavering after Piers's steady tone.

'Ah, poor lad – this come a hard blow, with your good mother still to mourn.'

'Not dead,' he insisted, shaking his head. 'Only it must be long – it must be long till he comes home . . .'

His voice died and he leant against Ursula.

'There now! He took swimey, poor child!' she cried. 'Fetch a sup of wine, Robin.'

It was Richard Medley who reached for the wine, poured it in his own cup and shoved it across the table. There was a terrible lassitude about all three men, as if they were drained by exhaustion and despair.

'Tell me!' Ursula said, holding the wine for the boy to drink.

'We rid these many days up coast and down and all along the shore,' Piers said. 'There – his colour's back. Rest now, cousin. Sit here by me. I am sorry you have naun but unhappy kinsmen come to comfort you.'

'Why the coast, sir?' Ursula asked, frowning.

'Many rid out of London thinking to see the battle. I saw clear, and so did my brother, how young Humfrey listened and fidgeted. I wanted him safe – so then I sent him on home ahead with your husband – but the lad slipped his care and was off.'

The wretched tale unfolded piece by miserable piece – how Robin Medley had roused from his sleep to find Humfrey and Agon both vanished – how one of the ostlers at the inn had told of two young gentlemen resting overnight before riding on 'to see the Spanish ships', how they had ridden out at first light – and then a third rider followed.

'So then I rode after,' Robin said, 'but never any sign of him. I'd bin a fool, I thought. Back I rid then, and met the rest at the forest pale – Master Piers and Master Richard, that is – the servants having to march it home since the horses was all sold ...'

When he heard Robin's tale, Piers had decided they must ride again to the coast, for he was too angry to believe a proper search had been made – and too angry to let Robin go home, either, though he was by then worn out.

'A fellow of these parts, a true foresty man, keeps an inn at the port,' Piers said, 'and so I sought him out. And there was Agon – well stabled, surelye, but not Humfrey Jolland alongside. And that man know well, as I know, too, that he's gone. For they let him sail in a boat taking out supplies, and that boat never come home – nor any in her's not been seen since save one – the ship's master got washed up, drowned, all of six mile down the shore.' He took his young kinsman's hand, saying sadly, 'This is a weary tale, dear lad, but had best be understood. Your brother is lost.'

The boy began to cry bitterly, then, but all the time shaking his head and saying, 'No! No!' in a miserable gulping voice.

Piers rose, saying that he could neither speak nor think any more till he had slept.

'Come home, brother. We're all jawled out and tomorrow must be another weary day. His father to tell . . .'

Ursula stood at the door and watched the brothers ride away home to Mantlemass. She had never before seen Master Piers looking as he looked now, defeated, his shoulders stooping, even in the saddle where usually he sat so straight. He was a man now in his late sixties, but ever upright, his grizzled hair still thick, as his father's had been – his brother, in fact, looked the older of the two.

The moon now hung behind low cloud that was little more than foggy, spreading a milky light. The two men, their tired horses perked up by the smell of home, merged soon into the distance and the stillness then was absolute. Nothing about the forest stirred or cried. So that Ursula, turning, went indoors with a soft tread, and as softly pulled the door behind her. Now she must face her husband and support him, for he lacked strength to support himself . . .

Young Jolland was halfway up the stair as she went indoors. He paused to look down at her, and they peered at one another through the light of the one big lantern hanging above the parlour door.

'Get to bed, child,' Ursula said. 'Sleep well. God keep you till morning.'

'And you also, cousin.' He smiled, or so she thought, but nervously. 'I am right. He'll come again another day.'

'For certain. Yes, yes – never a doubt. But go to your bed, now, do. I am truly weary.'

She watched him go. He would do better on his own, without his brother's bullying. Maybe he understood that, himself.

Ursula and Robin Medley had been husband and wife just a little less than six years. 'My love Robin,' 'my good love', she had often called him in that day book Mistress Susannah Mallory had encouraged her to keep. She had written it in those days somewhat laboriously, but now she was glad of a place where she might set down a little of her own thoughts and feelings. And now she wrote more coldly 'my husband'. After two years of marriage she had accepted that he was far less stable than any of them had supposed.

There was nothing Piers Medley had been unwilling to do for this son of a man he had once called friend then bitterly hated. No doubt it was partly to expiate that hatred that Piers had taken in his young son and daughter when they were orphaned. He never took any care to silence the 'slocksey talk' about the forest that the boy was in fact his secret son, and none the worse for that. Since he had never had any son of his own, and sorely regretted it, maybe Piers felt some pleasure in being thought Robin Medley's true father. He made no secret of the fact that Robin was heir to both Mantlemass and Ghylls Hatch.

Yet for all this, Robin Medley had never become true master of his own household. His nature seemed to run in two streams – the one lacking judgement, sharp and mean, the other still flashing out into the straightforward charm that had marked his boyhood. At those times he and Ursula could still find their old happiness; at others she knew he would always take the easy way to fortune, his view too short for sense. It was surely he who had persuaded Piers to dispose of more horses at one venture than could possibly be thought wise.

Once Ursula had written in her day book: 'He go his own way.' But then she had scratched it out carefully with a sharp knife, not wanting to admit, however secretly, that she knew he had some hidden life of his own . . .

He was still sprawled on the settle where she had left him. He was half asleep but roused when she came in.

'I did ever know,' he said, 'the day must come when I'd lose his trust.'

'Master Piers?' Ursula looked at him in sharp surprise. 'Have you so? He knows it were all no fault o' yourn.' She spoke slackly, without any true conviction.

'I slept like a hog in the straw. Save he were done-out wi' riding Agon I'd've got him home safe that same night.'

'Let be, Robin. Whose fault is little matter. I think most of his father – how Master Piers shall find words to tell him what come to his son.'

Robin groaned and put his face in his hands.

'Perk up, do!' she cried. 'Face it, in God's name. Leave groaning and crying . . . Best forget all till you've slept. Tomorrow'll come soon enough.'

She took his arms as if to tug him to his feet, and the

touch softened her. She put her arms round him in comfort, and he turned in relief. She spoke gently, forgetting her worries about him, and after a time he seemed to recover himself. At last she persuaded him to bed, helping him off with his dusty boots, laying his doublet neatly on the chest. He was half asleep already and fell into bed. She pulled up the covers and kissed him. He slept at once. She lay quietly beside him and saw the morning come as it was bound to do, beginning a day that could only be full of difficulty and distress.

That morning there returned the first three of the Mantlemass servants who had ridden to London and walked back. They had had a long march home, for Piers Medley had sent them to see the horses into their new quarters, not trusting to any agent buying for an absent master. So these three had travelled first north of London, and maybe the city had lured them to dally a shade longer on their way home. They came back with a swagger to impress their womenfolk and elders left behind.

'There's great houses and gentry in velvet and such, and pageants in the streets.'

'Ah, but you niver did see they beacons burn,' was the reply to that. 'A rare fine sight you missed!'

All that forenoon Ursula waited for word from Mantlemass but none came. At midday, she and her husband, with Roger Jolland, went on foot to Mantlemass to get their dinner there. It was the custom on three days of the week. The second three days, the Medley brothers were at Ghylls Hatch. On Sunday they might choose to dine in either house, according to circumstance and the meat supply, much depending on the season.

When Ursula and the others arrived at Mantlemass that day, Piers was listening to Henty, Bunce and Awcock, the returned servants. He looked up and smiled at the newcomers, but slightly, and took time to dismiss the men courteously before greeting the others.

'They're rare set-up,' he said. 'I could wish their masters had had as ramping a fine time!'

'You do still look weary, sir,' Ursula said, taking his hand and lifting it against her cheek.

'I slept ill. And must do so this many a long night.'

'Alas,' she said; and could say no more.

'What now?' Robin Medley said harshly. 'How'll we beard his father?'

'That's my burden. I'll be again to London, for the boy was my charge. Tomorrow, first light – but today I'll rest – today I feel an old man, which I never did till now.'

'I'll ride with you, then –'

'No, Robin, you will not. I'll take Will Bunce's grandson – he's the one shall ride with me. His eyes are round and out on his cheeks for hearing the others' London talk. It'll give him joy to sprug up and come-along.' He gave an impatient, troubled sigh. 'As well get some good from it all.'

No more was said. They went to table. Ursula half hoped her mother might have come to join them, as frequently she did, half feared what she must say of the manner of Humfrey's loss. She would for certain bait Robin sorely, and in his present state of mind he was unlikely to think much of courtesy.

But Lilias had not come. They ate a sombre meal, the table all but silent, the servants not daring to talk among themselves once the first dishes were cleared – as normally, at this table, they were accustomed. Ursula was preparing to leave for home, after a glance into the kitchens to see that all fared well, when Piers called her back.

'I have thought about the younger boy. Best I take him with me. Should it not be some comfort to his father? To see he's yet a son living? What d'you say to it?'

'Best here,' she said quickly. 'He's best here, surelye. Must he go home to a mother and a brother both lost? Let him be – pray let him be.'

'Aye – aye, if you think best. Take him, and I must spend hours more on the journeying. He's a poorish sort of mawkin.'

'His sorrow make him so – no more'n his sorrow . . .'

Piers smiled. 'I see he come your boy now.'

'I think so he is, sir. Well, I lost my first boy and now here's one already cut and stitched! Let me keep him as long as maybe. He'll be my eldest.'

'So be it, then,' Piers Medley agreed. 'It may well suit Sir Francis to leave him longer yet.' He embraced her warmly. 'You do give us all great love and care, my girl. That was a happy day you come to us – most happy.'

'Watch you ride wi' care, then, father,' Ursula said; she did not often give him the name, calling him more often *sir* or, in the older way, *master*. 'Bring yourself back home safe and soon – and quite whole; no bones broken from that wild way you do sometimes ride!'

They parted, and early next morning, as he had promised, Piers rode off with Will Bunce's grandson, Nat Penfold, in attendance. It was difficult for Nat to hold in his excitement and nervousness. But he went at the heels of a most unhappy man, and so he rode quiet and well-mannered, as his grandfather had sternly commanded.

A day or two after Piers left for London, Lilias Godman came to Mantlemass in search of Richard Medley.

'I rid by Plashets,' she told him. 'There's some trouble, looks like. Best you get down there and see what's doing.'

Richard had been busy about other matters. They had cropped early this year, but the last of the harvest was still to be got in. It was a bigger crop than usual, for they had sneaked a slice of land on their far boundary. Even one season's crop was not to be despised, and if they were obliged to be lawful and return the land to the forest, it would still have repaid the ploughing. This gave Richard Medley a quiet satisfaction, though he grinned to find himself as ready as any of his own tenants to snatch land from the forest's royal mistress. Mantlemass, long ago and by reason of a strange kinship now forgotten, had been a free gift from the Crown. The Medleys, who had inherited the place, knew themselves in a stronger position than most.

'Must it be yet?' Richard asked Lilias, unwilling to be distracted from the job in hand.

'Aye – better you go now. I see a lot o' mischief, all my days wi' iron – and I smell mischief now.'

With a hint of a groan, Richard shouted for his horse and rode off at once.

Soon it would be autumn. A heavy stillness hung like chains upon the forest, birds were at the brambles, the ground stained with their purple droppings. Richard rode slowly, reluctant to find trouble, never too good at dealing hardly, and as always vaguely uneasy in the absence of his brother. Richard Medley's life had spent itself about the forest and he had wanted no different – he could easily count the times he had travelled the fifty odd miles to London. His misformed shoulder had made him a diffident boy, and though he had thrown off his worry as he grew older, now again in later life he felt it as a burden. It had deprived him, through his own honesty, of wife and children. He commanded his men at Plashets, the iron working where he had long been master, less by firmness than by gentleness. They all knew him there, had known his father, and he seldom needed to raise his voice.

But as he neared the place today he more than half knew what he must contend with.

'It will be the matter of the ore,' he muttered, needing the comfort of his own voice.

There was a load long due from a digging further south – payment of an old debt from a fellow master. It was needed now, but had had to be asked for twice. It should have come two weeks earlier, weather conditions being favourable for the removal and cartage. Richard had sent a third time to speak of the delay and his man would be just about returned.

The track ran into a good clearing just short of the workings, a green shelf of land, kept fair by overflow from the nearby pond. A knot of men were gathered there, clustering round one of their number – a redhead Richard easily recognized. He was one of the Hentys. His father and uncles and their families had worked either at Plashets or at Strives Minnis, but this one, Thomas, had been about other ventures before returning to the forest. This set him a little apart; in spite of his name and his family, he bore the mark of other places, knowing too much, very ready to display the fact, and much inclined to spark rebellion among the younger workers.

Richard paused, looking down. At that same moment one of the older men punched Thomas Henty on the chin. His head went up and he went reeling back. He was caught by his nearest neighbour – who instantly shoved him hard against the next man. Someone laughed, but then there was silence. Henty tried to right himself, but he was given no chance to recover. Each struck out, shoving him away, so that he was buffeted from one to another, at first spun round the quickly formed ring, then shoved

harder from side to side. Giddied and stumbling, he tried to cover his head with his hands, pulling his cap down over his ears, but having it tweaked off and sent flying. The ring opened wider all the time, so that every blow sent the wretched victim staggering further, until at last his legs gave and he went sprawling on the ground. Someone's boot swung, but at that moment Richard rode on towards them. The man who had started it all then called off the pack.

'Wait, you! Mus' Richard come.'

Richard dismounted and a lad ran to take his bridle. He walked forward in silence into the circle of blackbrowed men and stood briefly looking down at Henty, whose face was puffing, both eyes closed, blood running from his nose and from a cut above the left brow.

'What now?' Richard asked.

'They set about me! The sworly beggering lot o' grummuts! They was all set on to kill me!'

'Why so? What had you done to 'em?'

At that a great clamour broke out. The men clustered round Richard, shouting out what Thomas Henty had done.

'Ask'm where the ore goo!'

'That's a man serve two masters – let'm tell where the load rest now!'

'Where's his new master bide – ask'm that!'

'And who pay'm? And how much? And where that come to we'm waiting for these long days?'

Richard held up his hand and they were silent, voices trailing away.

'Best speak up, Thomas Henty,' Richard said. 'I thought once before this you could've played me false. Speak out, then. There'll be fair judgement – you know that and all here know that.'

The man looked at Richard from his bloody eyes and his swollen mouth contrived to spit.

'That's for Plashets – and rot all!' he snarled . . .

When Richard, that evening at supper, spoke of this to Lilias Godman, who was at table, he blamed himself for dealing badly with the business.

'I made a sore boffle. There's an enemy for all time – to Plashets, to Mantlemass. I should'a treated more carefully.'

'There's no good way to dally, come the moment's hot.'

'I did forget he had so young a wife.'

'I doubt you treated such with any great harshness, Master Richard.'

'Let you seek who paid, I told him. I sent him away – no quarter. He took what he owned in a little cart. The wife and two little 'uns walked alongside. She never looking back and the children crying. Last of all, the old lame span'l, not knowing what should ever be next.' He sighed.

'Well then – all's done with and may be forgot. Save only that the ore's lost. Where?'

'T'other side the forest, so they tell. Not overseas, which is a wonder.'

'A wonder indeed – and not likely true. Who're you to know where it shall end? The Spanish are not gone for ever – they'll come again. And just as always, they'll come first a-filching of our iron – like the Dutch and the French and every other sort and kind.'

'Maybe now there shall be peace,' Ursula said. 'Peace and prosperity, God willing.'

'Peace and prosperity, daughter? Never think it. For us as works the iron, peace did never mean prosperity. It's war – guns – gunstones that fill our pockets.'

'There's other trade,' Richard said. 'Not each and every ship sails to battle, nor every man's a soldier. With fighting done, a man turns quickly to ploughing and harrowing. What d'you say, Robin?'

'I'm bound to horses, will I, nil I. So there's iron for shoes and nails and bits and spurs – what should I care?'

Richard smiled and turned to young Jolland, hoping to rally him, for he had barely spoken since Master Piers set out for London. 'What's your consideration of this matter, cousin?'

The boy shook his head, looking to Ursula for help.

'Our cousin tell me there'll come more ships out of Spain,' she said. 'But I'll not hear of it.'

'Not yet,' he said. 'One day. Not yet.'

Lilias frowned. 'That's slack talk, daughter. It's ill to encourage him. Best such things be forgot.'

'But he mean what he tell, mother. Didn't he say about his brother?'

'Let it go,' Richard said, looking uneasily from mother to daughter. They were well matched. Ursula's first resistance had come when she married as she chose, not as her mother had decided; resistance had grown in her since then. Iron ran in Lilias's veins and so for sure it must run in Ursula's, and indeed it could be seen.

'Peace, peace – at Mantlemass if nowhere else in all the world!' Richard cried – and filled Lilias's wine cup to distract her. 'I wish my brother might return – he has a deedy errand and I think of him. I never did feel my easy self in this place wi'out him.'

'As do none of us, surelye,' Lilias said, setting her sharpness by and with that reserved fondness that always took her when she spoke of Piers Medley. Piers alone had won Lilias over to the marriage of Robin and Ursula – but how and what it was that had changed Lilias so entirely at that time he had never discovered. Considering Ursula's husband now, Richard Medley did wonder a little if it had all been for the best.

As Richard set about placating Lilias and interposing his own good humour between mother and daughter, Robin himself said nothing. He sat slackly in his place, slightly grinning, as if by no means unwilling to see his wife in conflict with her mother. A poor sort of courtesy, Richard thought.

'There'll be a deal to do come my brother returns, Robin. So many horses sold at one sweep – I wonder were that altogether masterly.'

Ursula put in swiftly, 'I did so wonder, sir.'

'No matter for women to make-and-mend,' Robin said.

'There's women and women.' Lilias perversely shifted ground to defend her daughter. 'She say as much to me when you all rid off to London. So many, she say. I wonder is that wisdom.'

'The Master know his own business, madam,' her son-in-law replied.

They sat long at table in the small parlour to which, since they had become so few, the Medleys had gradually retreated and now had most of their being. At Ursula's side, young Jolland had fallen asleep. The candles burnt low, the conversation dwindled. They all waited for Lilias to rise and say her goodnights, but she remained, sipping her wine and seeming in no hurry to leave. It was Ursula who said at last,

'Mother – it is time and more that you got safe home.'

At this the boy stirred and looked up, alert as a leveret, crying out,

'Are they here? Are they here?'

'Does he think still o' the Spanish?' Lilias asked. 'No, my good young sir, all are fled.'

He rubbed his eyes and looked foolish. 'I dreamt . . .'

'Let that set you to better ways, then. To sleep at your host's table, indeed! The young are like brutes in our time. Fie on you, young Jolland – remember courtesy though you forget all lessons else.'

He said, 'Yes, madam,' and instantly slept again.

'His father shall think poorly of his country manners, daughter. Best you see him corrected.'

'Mother,' said Ursula again, 'it is time you were home.'

Mention of the boy's father troubled her. What if he sent at once to fetch the child away? She did not want to lose him. He seemed to her, fancifully no doubt, like some strange messenger, one needing succour to sustain him in a nameless task.

So when two days later, Agnes Goodale came seeking her where she was resting in the last afternoon sun, Ursula could not like her news.

'The Master is home to Mantlemass,' Agnes said, 'and ask for you, madam. And Sir Francis Jolland has rid back wi' him from London.'

4

Sir Francis

Ursula rose at once, saying, 'I'll fetch my cousin.'

'Shalln't I seek him, lady?'

'I know where he'll have hid.'

'Tell me and I'll goo – let you take more care.'

'Oh be silent, Agnes!' Ursula snapped. 'Let be! I say what I'll do and you shall do what I tell you and no more.'

She heard her mother's voice ringing through her own and flushed slightly. But she was too concerned to draw back and Agnes's stricken expression and quickly filled eyes were merely irritating.

'Go tell Master Piers I'm bringing the boy soon's I may.'

She did not wait to watch Agnes obey, but went at once across the court and by way of a narrow track out on to the forest. The warm clear day had been as pleasant as midsummer, but the faintest chill beneath the sunlight had set a haze over the distance. Soon must come those days when more and more birds in long trails and streamers would divide the sky, moving to distances that none about these parts could name. Then in the emptied sky would remain none but the commonplace – and among them the faithful swans.

As a sop to Agnes, who was sensible enough, Ursula picked her way with care where falling bracken caught at her hem and her ankles. She came at last to a small and narrow ghyll where a little river's waters emptied into a small pond before chasing out to drop sharply over a rocky ledge. The ledge itself could not be seen at this season, for it was obscured by the last wild flourishing of hartstongue and briar and woodbine. The sound of the water dropping made the whole place sleepy with its rhythm, endless and improvident. The pond had been larger once, so Piers had told her; they had fished there as boys and later. Neglected, it had broken its banks in winter, losing its form, wearing away a deeper channel with the force of its flow over the ledge. Soon it might vanish altogether under the encroaching underwood, becoming a mysterious, a hidden force.

At the water's edge Ursula paused. She saw no one. But she knew he must be there, as she knew by now many other things about him; as that his certainty of his brother's return moved him more to dread than to delight. She spoke quietly, not calling out, but saying in her everyday voice, 'Cousin . . .?'

At once there was a rustling somewhere above her. She looked up and saw the boy peering from the branches of a young oak – he sat among them like a fly on a toadstool, so shapely was the tree.

'Come down to me and I'll speak with you,' Ursula said.

'Master Piers is home?'

'I'll see you clim down – then I'll answer.'

'Tell me your news.' Roger Jolland said, swinging down obediently enough.

'You spoke true. Master Piers is home. Nor he's not rid back alone.'

He said cautiously, 'Not?'

'Nay – there's another come along. Why else'd I tramp through the brakes to flush you from hiding?'

'My father.'

'Surelye! Your father – your good father, come all this way. And in sore grief, I doubt it not. Oh you must give him comfort, child!'

'I know what he will say. That he will take me home.'

Ursula checked at his expression, knowing too well that his dismay was reflected in her own face. But it must be as Sir Francis chose – and if he had indeed lost one son, for sure he would cling the harder to what remained.

'Come now,' she said, and set her arms about the boy to draw him along with her.

'Is he alone, cousin Ursula?'

'I tell you I have not seen him, but bustled to find you and tell you your good news.'

'Old Ned did never let my father ride alone. For sure he'll be come. And Lance! And Lance's son, Gil, maybe.'

'Hurry, then, and see for yourself.'

He caught her hand and hung on to it with both his own.

'Never let him take me away with him! I must be here – I cannot tell why – but I know. I must be here when my brother comes back. Don't send me away.'

She replied sharply, distressed for both of them.

'It is not for me to send but for Sir Francis to take. Hurry, now! You tug and pull and pout like some lumpish baby.'

But she kept his hand in hers, and now it seemed a long way to Mantlemass. She began to wish she had let Agnes do her errand after all. There could have been none of this parleying and delay . . .

Piers Medley and his guest were in the hall when

Ursula and Roger at last reached Mantlemass.

'Here now, sir,' Piers cried at once, 'they are here!' He set his arm about Ursula and led her to the stranger. 'My good daughter, Sir Francis. She has brought you your own dear son.'

The boy started forward, then hesitated. His father had not yet glanced at him, but had moved to Ursula, taking her hand, saying,

'We are cousins, cousin – and so I salute you.'

Then smiling a little through his grave manner, he bent towards her and kissed her on the brow.

Ursula neither smiled nor frowned, nor moved forward, nor moved away. She stood with her chin a little lifted, her hand still in his, as if examining his face and judging what might be found there – the eyes grey, the mouth firm, above a neat beard. His brow was broad and generous but at this time furrowed, almost knotted with worry and grief. She would have given much to touch his forehead, to smooth away his cares and bring him content . . .

Her impulse confused her and she looked down and stepped back a little, drawing her hand from his and pulling Roger into her place.

'I am keeping you from your son, sir . . .'

She watched the boy still hesitate – then fling himself into his father's arms, breaking into tears as he found himself enfolded. She felt Piers's hand on her shoulder. She seemed then to hear her own voice as she and the boy watched the swans fly over – *They mate for life, as we do . . .*

In the few moments since she had stepped indoors her own life had changed its course.

Almost overnight came the end of summer; the knowledge of winter was behind the steady bustle that occupied both households. But at Mantlemass the guest and his troubles

took precedence even over the yearly round. At this time in his late thirties, Sir Francis was handsome without vanity, strong without harshness. He had the courtesy of selflessness, as with any true and honest gentleman, and there was nothing Piers Medley would not do to help him in his trouble.

So together they rode to the coast, retracing every inch that Piers had already found empty of all hope. Again they sought out those already spoken to – boatmen, solitary dwellers by the shore, hearing all the same words, save for the fact that the wreckage of *Seabird* had been washed up on that season's highest tide. They spoke to the landlord at the inn, who had found Humfrey Jolland a place in the boat – and wept, now, to recall it.

'It come too hard to curb his young spirit, sir. That were a day o' days and not the match o' any other in my whole life. I stayed to think too little.'

'Aye, indeed, you stayed to think too little,' Sir Francis answered, bitterly.

'There was high promise in him,' said the landlord. And this was when he covered his face and turned away.

'Let it rest,' Sir Francis muttered. He put his hand briefly on the man's shoulder. 'God ordered that day in this as in all else. Be at peace, then. No blame.'

So once again with heavy hearts they rode home.

Ursula was indoors at Ghylls Hatch and looking from the window, holding young Simon in her arms to show him how the leaves were tumbling golden off the shivering birches. She saw the small cavalcade as it moved along the skyline and called out to Roger.

'They're home. Run to greet your father.'

'He is thinking of Humfrey.'

'He must think now of you, surelye. See you regard him well. Grow like him and you grow as his son should.'

Agnes Goodale, who was nearby, folding and smoothing linen to put in the press, looked up over the pile mounting on the table between them. Ursula met the glance as she spoke to Roger. Neither woman wavered. Only the slightest warm curve of smile broke the smoothness of Agnes's always untroubled face. But it was message enough. Ursula had hoped for a confidante, for this very one, indeed, and now the decision was taken. Goodales had served before at Mantlemass and Ghylls Hatch – and surely Master Piers had once spoken of some remote family connection? Then, Agnes should be the kinswoman Ursula had lacked . . .

Francis Jolland lingered at Mantlemass. If any wished him gone it could have been Robin Medley, who occupied himself with Ghylls Hatch business to the extent of being from home as much as he was able. Francis's grief had been a heavy burden on all of them. Not that he imposed it, but that they felt it for him, respecting his silences, his clear inability to rouse himself. He rode much about the forest, or walked there slowly and alone. Those who lived and worked in these parts grew accustomed to seeing him, some glad to let their sympathy be known by their respectful greetings – others, too shy or slow even to confront him, turning off the track and slipping as neat as deer into the deeper forest.

At the end of one late September day, Ursula being at supper at Mantlemass, but without her husband, Sir Francis spoke of her mother.

'This very forenoon, I was her visitor. She is a woman of much wisdom and I am the better for my time in her company.'

'I am glad of it, sir. What did she offer that were so wise?'

'Why, she told me that God beats at men as men beat

at iron. And when all's finished, the iron – so it be of good ore – makes a better shape from such hammering. And so it is with men.'

'She'll say what she choose. No matter who to.'

'Very rightly so. And I answered her with due respect, I promise you. But what if the ore be faulty, I asked her. What twisted fearful thing may come from the fire?'

'What then? What did my mother say then?'

He smiled. 'Ah – she assured me she was a judge of ore and of men – and that I might do well enough.'

'I am sorry if she seemed bold.'

This time he laughed. 'I was eager to accept such comfortable flattery ... And when I say so I am not mocking your mother – but myself!'

From this moment the mood lightened, the misery wore away. Sir Francis, it was clear, had accepted his loss and would now keep quieter mourning. They moved at this time, too, into a spell of days with bright sun and sharply blue skies. It was, they said, St Luke's little summer come a few weeks early; and a time when much could be done about farm and pasture and forest that would otherwise have to wait right round until the next spring.

For Ursula these calm fair days were full of turmoil. She was for ever avoiding encounters with Francis Jolland – yet for ever seeking him out. She longed for his departure, dreaded never seeing him again. And though she prayed daily for forgiveness, and wept at her own sinful heart, she could not be rid of a rising resentment against the child she carried, so hopelessly marking her as a wife. Yet this, too, was a confusion of thought and feeling, for like many another woman at such times she was shining and blooming with good health and energy. She thought how she had dreamt of her children, and once had written their names in her day book – Piers and Cecily, Lewis and

Roger; perhaps Edmund – she had written this last with a query following. Piers had been stillborn, and Cecily had turned out to be Simon, but she had never found herself able to alter the list she had written in those first days of her marriage. They stood for an innocent happiness and confidence that was now lost. Sometimes, allowing her fancy its head, she would write of 'my son Piers' as if he had lived, and was now grown and moving beside her … So in this same mood, unable to resist the delight of seeing his name on the page before her, she wrote over and over *Francis* … *Francis* … But this she cut from the book and threw into the fire. It was not for such entries that Susannah Mallory had urged her to keep the book, but for future generations, she had said, to learn of their forebears …

In these days won from the approaching winter, Ursula would get herself up on to the old broad-backed pony, Dapple, and go at a walking pace through the forest to visit her mother.

At once, young Jolland would appear, calling,

'Wait! I'll see you safe.'

He walked beside her, then, his hand on the bridle, half protective, half needing protection. And often they found the boy's father ahead of them at Strives, as Ursula had known well they might, sitting in the sun on the bench along the wall of the house, with Lilias Godman easy at his side.

'There sit our two gossips!' Ursula said to Roger, on one such day. 'They talk fit to set the world to rights.'

The pair were conversing deeply and earnestly – she with the hard-won wisdom of her greater years, he with the learning that knows well how to accept such wisdom, Ursula marvelled that her mother could so hold the attention of a man whose life had touched even on the difficult fringes of court and government, as his family's had done for generations. He would speak, Ursula believed, as straightly to the Queen herself as to Lilias Godman, and to Lilias Godman with as much courtesy as to the Queen.

'Father!' called Roger, running forward.

Sir Francis rose and came towards his son, but looking beyond him. He cuffed the boy about the head, though with smiles, crying out,

'Fie, boy – remember your manners! Are you not squiring the lady?'

By then Ursula had reached the plat before the house. Roger ran to hold the rein again. His father, without ceremony, lifted Ursula from the saddle and set her on her feet. She did not thank him, but with a quick unlooking smile walked past him to her mother and gave her some silly, merry greeting.

'Watch not to be oversturdy, daughter,' Lilias said. 'How often must I say it? Seeing you lost one already, you take too little care, seems me.'

'Oh be silent, mother!' Ursula cried, flushed crimson with anger and confusion. 'D'you think I am a babe unborn myself? Let be.'

Lilias pulled down the corners of her mouth.

'How our children do plague us, Sir Francis. There's little kindness in the young and little to hope for of love and gratitude.'

'And so, madam, have I heard my own father say. It is a parent's cry, see you – it shall echo, no doubting, from these days to the end of time!'

'Lord save us – and God be thanked I'll be gone from this world before manners and decency do crumble away.'

Such talk led them into laughter, and Ursula was able to recover her temper.

When she rose to go, Sir Francis rose too. They returned through the forest together, he walking beside her, leading his own horse.

'Pray ride on,' she said. 'I should not delay you.'

'No, no – it is good to walk. The boy shall run ahead and tell of our coming soon. Off with you,' he cried to his son. He watched him out of sight, and sighed. 'How hard shall it go with him that I make a different heir?'

'Must you so?'

'I cannot see this lad in my cruel world, cousin.' He seemed to shrug away the problem, as if he found it unbearable. 'When do you next visit your good mother?'

'Why – any day.'

'Let it be tomorrow.'

He looked up at her, his expression unflurried; sad, rather, and gentle.

Ursula said, forcing the words, 'When shall you return to London?'

'No doubt but it should be soon.'

She did not answer, only nodded.

'I have no will to leave here. Which is, no doubt, best reason why I should.'

'Yes,' she said, barely heard, 'it is fully time.'

Then they proceeded in silence, for everything had been said.

In the big pasture above and behind the Ghylls Hatch stabling and mews, they were schooling a young chestnut. As Ursula and Francis Jolland approached they looked up and away and saw the horse and the men like figures in a graceful dance, capering and cavorting with a rhythm so strong and faultless it seemed almost as if pipe and tabor kept time.

Then the picture broke as Roger came running towards them up the bank, that slight falter from his lame foot threatening to trip him, he came so eagerly.

'That's Fair Ruby they're schooling. Do you see who it is, cousin?'

'You see more'n I do,' Ursula answered, smiling at him. She said to his father, 'He has a quick eye. He must be sad to leave us here, I do think.'

At once she wished the words back. She had spoken of a plain enough topic – the return home of a visitor – maybe to distract from a sensation of increasing danger. But the boy's manner changed instantly and alarmingly. He ran to her side, laying his hands on Dapple's bridle and straining at it as if he would rein in the cantering of time itself.

'Cousin! Cousin! Let me stay! Sir – father – I must stay! I must stay!'

'Peace, peace,' his father said. 'No doubt but you shall come here another time.'

'I am bound to stay! My brother will come back! I must be here!'

'Say no more, boy! You are troubling me and I have troubles enough. Your brother is lost. Only madness thinks otherwise ... Now – we'll see the lady safe indoors – then back with us to Mantlemass. I see too well it is time we both left this place.'

Yet a week later he still stayed. No more had been said of his departure, nor any word been spoken about the boy's protest. But they all saw how Francis Jolland now watched his son, taking more time to be with him, walking and riding with him, talking to him earnestly and long.

'A loving father,' Ursula wrote – and took her knife and scratched away the words as she had scratched others in the past. She told herself she wished him gone.

The movement about the forest was all of passage and departure, of farewell. Early and late came the sound of journeying geese, the winter riding at their backs.

Only the swans, of all the morning fliers, still returned at evening. Ursula thought miserably as she looked up at them, 'I am less in honour than they . . .'

On a rainy day, somewhere about dusk, Piers Medley rode down the track from Mantlemass and found Ursula by her own hearth. She was sitting at a small table, with a thick leather bound book before her, a full inkhorn to hand and a new cut pen.

She rose to greet him, and he kissed her cheek. Then he pushed her down gently into her chair and pulled himself a stool, so that he sat facing her.

'I rid this way at this time to speak of the Jollands, daughter Ursula.'

'Yes, sir?' She chose another quill and began to sharpen it, giving the task her close attention.

'Come the father leave us, shall you be ready to see the son left behind?'

She looked up at once and her answer was in her face for him to read.

'Is it spoken of, then?'

'It is. But Sir Francis must have your sure consent, or there's nothing shall be decided. We spoke a long while of it. Sir Francis must return within the week – he's doddled here all too long, so he say. But could stay for ever and be content, he tell me and my brother.' Piers smiled, pleased at what he saw as a compliment, unaware of how intently Ursula looked at her hands. 'I think the boy could be content, too.'

'Aye. He will be. And so shall I.'

'Best he be here wi' you at Ghylls Hatch.'

'Indeed. Yes. Best he be here.'

'And Robin . . .?' Piers sounded unusually tentative. Who was to know, these days, which way Robin Medley might jump?

'He shall think so too, surelye,' said Ursula, so firm that Piers smothered a smile.

'It will be till spring at least. Come spring, Sir Francis shall return and maybe fetch his lad away.'

'In the spring,' she said.

'I doubt he'll ever be his father's heir, Ursula. Our cousin see the boy to be somewhat a weakling – truly he look pretty peaked and pathery at times. And then there's his seeing . . . Who's to know if that be some softness in his poor brain?'

'The next brother, then? He shall be heir?'

'Why, it can happen, that I do know,' Piers answered. 'When my father lost his eldest son, though not by death, thank God, yet he named me then his eldest and so I was heir to him.'

'But had he named your younger brother, sir – what then?'

He laughed. 'There speaks my shrewd girl! A sore trial to my vanity, that had bin. But, my good soul, I'll be vainer and say I were five times the man young Jolland seem to be.'

'*Five* times, Master Piers?'

'Twice, then,' he said laughing. 'But ten times as old! Well, then, I'll tell our cousin it shall be well. And that he shall be welcome when he come again. Shall I say so? That you did say so?'

'Aye. Say so. In the spring. We'll look for him in the spring.'

It seemed a long time.

5

Ursula

Short of Christmas, Ursula had her third son, just as Roger Jolland had promised – and as she had promised she told him he should stand sponsor at the christening.

'But we'll call him by his second name, and that shall be Lewis. Otherly, how shall I know one son Roger from the next?'

The child was no more than four hours old, but Ursula's bed was surrounded by her family. Lilias was there, and Piers and Richard Medley, young Jolland, Agnes Goodale who had delivered the baby, and two of the maids from Mantlemass who had come running when they heard the news.

'Stand back!' Agnes insisted, happy and officious. 'Let the lady breathe new air!'

Agnes was a great one for new air. She had flung the bedchamber window wide as soon as the child was born, and had held him there a second or two in a manner utterly scandalous to Lilias Godman. But, Agnes insisted, her mother and her grandmother had ever done so, and never any harm. To open the window after a death seemed reasonable to Lilias – but after a birth . . . !

'He look on the world, madam, and know his place,' Agnes said firmly. 'It should be so done.'

Now the window was safe shut against the winter, the room was snug, the baby sleeping. Already the struggle was almost forgotten and his mother lay happy and at rest.

Only the child's father was absent, having gone off to the town at this same hour yesterday and not returned. He rode in as Piers and Richard left Ghylls Hatch and turned for home.

'Laggard!' Piers shouted at him. 'Get indoors and see what your wife has brought you!'

Robin only waved and rode on round to the stables.

'He heard naun. The wind's in his ears,' Richard Medley said quickly, seeing his brother's face.

'Maybe so, maybe no,' Piers answered. 'I've asked too much of him, could be. Great promise, little fulfilment . . . Well, many are so. We think too much he's a Medley. He is not. His father's blood show in him now.'

As the brothers rode on to Mantlemass, Robin was entering the house and finding his way to his wife's bedside. He glanced into the cradle and grimaced, then said, not quite teasingly enough,

'I see you're set-on to stay the only woman in this family.' He stooped towards the baby and ran one fingertip under its chin. 'That's a lad even by his jaw line!'

'Oh husband – did you wish a daughter? Why, how should I ha' known it, come you niver asked me for one? What a petition I might've made all these months!'

'Next time . . .' he said.

'Lord, lord!' she cried, laughing but with a note of recognizable bitterness. 'I barely rid myself – and you cry *Next time*! You've to stay at home more, then, sir.'

'If I'd cantered Fair Ruby home in last night's darks

you'd have scolded just as sore ... And Master Piers'd've had my head for certain.'

'It were Emerald carried you to town, husband.'

'Well – there's a nag as needs care, if ever I see. One stumble and he's down and me with'm. Little you care for your husband's neck – and that the only one he's like to have.'

'You'd have risked it once!' she cried.

Now they were both laughing, but emptily; there was no humour or tenderness in the sound. Ursula's eyes had long ago filled with tears, and now they rolled wretchedly down on to the coverlet. The excitement and relief of the birth had sustained her, body and spirit, but now she felt so weary she thought she could never find strength to wipe her tears away.

'Ah now – in the good Lord's name,' Robin groaned.

'Tell Agnes come here ...'

'Ursula! It were teasing!'

'I give you a lovely boy and you fret and fume and think only of the next I'll fetch out for you! Best I had died!'

'Dear Lord,' he muttered again. 'It was a *jest*!'

'Agnes – fetch Agnes ...'

Agnes, however, must have been waiting at the door, for she came running before ever the call was made, all soothing and solacing.

'Let us be, sir! Go now. What a tumult! Poor soul – to see her weeping at such a time! And fit to curdle and dry the milk in her breast.'

She bent over Ursula, enveloping her, excluding the clumsy fool, indignation with the father competing in her voice with consolation of the mother.

'There, my dear soul, there ... Oh the things men never will learn!'

'How should I tell it were a girl he wanted?'

'Now there's a tale,' scoffed Agnes. 'What father ever asked for daughters? We know that – as were daughters ourselves. He's but mocked you, lady – give him leave. They're a mocking lot o' grummuts, men – ever so and ever shall be!'

'Mockery was not in it!' Robin Medley cried, all but shouting.

A sad scene for a birth chamber, Agnes called it, when she had finally packed him off.

Later he returned and knelt by the bedside, and made his peace. Ursula smiled and he smiled back, but neither was sincere. Presently he went off whistling and she had no notion when she might see him next – that evening, or a week ahead. She was left to brood over the way their marriage went, how from that first heady romance that had seemed to promise the world, the dream had blurred, had faded and now was gone. Maybe it was so with all marriages, but she had little means of judging. Her mother had been a widow so long that Ursula had forgotten her father. As for the Medleys, Piers had lost his wife after little more than a year, and however his life had gone since, he had not married again. As for his younger brother, for reasons of honour he had not married at all. Ursula had watched many of the girls who worked about Mantlemass and Ghylls Hatch, had seen them bloom and then fade and grow haggard as life became sterner. She had supposed, as no doubt they, too, had done, that it must be different for her.

She had time to think, in the time after the birth, for she took longer to recover than seemed usual or sensible. And lying alone in the big bed she thought most not of Robin, not of the husband her mother had wanted for her, but of another yet, telling herself she sinned but finding no willingness to repent. What she dreamt of she knew she could never have; there was no need to renounce a joy so distant and intangible.

On the Sunday after the birth, the baby would be carried down to Staglye village, to be baptized in the parish church by the parish priest – no longer Father this or that, as for so many years, but the Reverend somebody, whom nobody quite knew as yet, whose name they somehow failed or refused to remember. As often in the past, when the faith of the country changed its tone, the people of these withdrawn places held their peace, prayed their own prayers, and looked at the ground. For the first time in all the long years at Mantlemass, the parish priest was absent from table on Sundays for dinner, remaining below in the village, and suffering none quite knew what lonely deprivations. Piers Medley never could decide where his feelings lay in this matter. He deplored a break with custom as he had known it from childhood; yet he was not particularly regretful at being free of the last incumbent, God rest him, who had grown very tedious and fumbling, spilling his food and his wine before falling asleep over bones most inadequately picked – Well, there had to be change, and some was for the better. When he came to such thoughts, Piers Medley would remember his grandmother, Dame Cecily Mallory, whom he had dearly loved, and recall her wondering delight when first she read the Bible in English . . .

No one was troubled at the thought of the baby, a few days old, travelling through winter weather to the cold church, since he would be especially in God's keeping on such an occasion. Happily the tracks were dry and hard. Agnes would carry the baby, riding slow old Dapple, while Roger Jolland led him the four or so miles, and the child's father rode ahead at a walking pace. Then there would be

Piers and Richard Medley in attendance, and the grandmother, Lilias Godman. Many servants and neighbours would follow, returning to celebrate with feasting and gifts.

'Who are the godparents?' Lilias demanded, on the eve of the christening. 'You have spoken never a word of the godparents, daughter.'

'Cousin Jolland shall be godfather. A promise I made him long ago.'

'He's little more'n a child – and a strange child.'

'Let this solemn office steady him, then.'

'And the godmother? I see no suitable woman in this place of men. I know no law says a grandmother mayn't stand sponsor.'

'The godmother shall be Agnes,' Ursula said.

She flicked a glance at her mother and saw Lilias shut her mouth very hard and tight. Master Piers had come visiting and sat now over by the hearth. He looked across at the two women, saying nothing, smiling a little into his beard.

'Shall it indeed be so, daughter?'

'Aye, mother. It shall. And no ill word to it.'

'I find it strange.'

'Why – what do you ask in such a case – save honesty and God-fearing and a good loyal heart? I'd sooner any one than riches, be they given now or after death.'

Lilias said, in that gentry voice she could still use when the occasion seemed to call for it,

'How says the master of Mantlemass?'

Ursula knew that Piers had smoothed away his smile, but knew there was nothing mocking in it. He replied solemnly.

'Why, that the child's mother must choose, madam.'

'And is it not true, sir,' Ursula said quickly, 'that

Goodales might call kin wi' Medleys?'

'Why – yes, perhaps. If they so chose. But it'd be but a faint mew of a call.'

'How so?' Lilias demanded, incredulous.

'I have forgot persizely,' he replied. 'But there's few of us in these parts live altogether to ourselves. Did you never hear that my father's mother was a Bostel? Bostels, then, are servants and kin, both, but make little of it. If once so, then again. It'll not be the last time Goodales and Medleys come together – or so I'd reckon.'

Lilias muttered that Agnes was a sight too perked up already, and to be godmother to a son of the household must make her unbearably stomachy.

'Agnes is a friend to me,' Ursula said. 'So – let's hear no more.'

'Strange times we see,' said Lilias, for the sake of the last word. Then changing the subject quickly, she asked Master Piers what enterprise carried Robin Medley so often past Strives Minnis and on along that track that quitted the forest by the farthest gate in the pale, then joined the old road to the town.

Ursula was aware that there was the barest, almost startled hesitation, before Piers answered.

'Hoads at Rushy Ghyll've a black stallion fit for Fair Ruby. Someone of us needs be watching his paces if they're to put her to him, her next season.'

'You did decide it should be Sultan for her,' Ursula said, not thinking long enough.

'Aye,' he agreed patiently, 'but any man may change his mind.'

No more was said.

That year went over as fast as any other. The stirring and the tragic events of the summer slipped so completely into the past that they were all but forgotten. It was Christmas, it was Epiphany; Distaff Sunday was dutifully kept, as always here; Twelfth Night sent Christmas packing and the New Year became the urgent responsibility of all. Master Richard took young Jolland under his wing and rode him about the forest, keeping him days on end at Plashets, encouraging, unobtrusively teaching, smiling at the boy's response, at first slow and grudging, then turning to interest, to eagerness.

In his first months, the new baby prospered, his brother Simon was sickly, weeks together. Roger Jolland carved toys for both children and it was the baby's fist that seemed to grasp at them the firmer. This was surely a clever, promising child, showing his mettle already. Yet so, at first, had Simon appeared. Frowning and biting her lip, Ursula stared at the older brother as he slept, flushed and breathing badly.

'My sister Lucy was just so,' Robin Medley assured his wife. 'Very dwiney and lear, she was. I do recall that well. Think of her now – so pink and plump.'

Ursula smiled a little, distracted by the mention of Lucy, her girlhood's playmate.

'I wish she'd not gone so far. No word for a year at a time. Oh I remember well how we did gabble and babble together in those old times!'

'And I remember, of that time, the day your mother tell you'd gone from the forest, and should wed where she chose – and she'd not choose me.'

'Is that what you remember?' She was touched. Perhaps, after all, she had mistaken the change in him?

'Aye – and the world all but ended!' Then he burst into loud and mocking laughter, destroying the hopeful moment, sneering at the eager boy he had been. 'Young lads take life hard. As well we learn to change!'

Ursula said sharply, 'My mother tells me you ride by Strives often – but not to speak wi' her. She wonders why.'

'Hoads of Rushy Ghyll have a fine stallion worth the watching,' he answered instantly. 'Master Piers seek a stud for Fair Ruby.'

And so indeed Master Piers had said. Yet Ursula felt that he had warned her husband of questions possibly to be asked, and had supplied a glib answer to be used. 'I told them such-and-such,' he would have said. 'Do you answer thus-and-thus.' No doubt he had supposed Robin to be in pursuit of some willing forest girl.

'What'd you think?' he demanded, aware of her hesitation. 'That I went a-visiting my doxy?'

She flushed slightly but stayed obstinate.

'I'd never take the Strives track to visit Hoads. And so, no doubt, my mother did think.'

'Your mother have four pair o' eyes to her head.' He leant towards Ursula roughly, thrusting out his chin. 'And shall I tell you – shall I? – why I ride that way?'

'Aye – aye, do, come you've reason.'

'My home lie down that track.'

Ursula was utterly bewildered. He had never in all the years ever spoken of any such place. Once or twice lately he had seemed to her to speak strangely, but never so strangely as this.

'What home?' she cried. 'Here is your home. Ghylls Hatch is your home. All Mantlemass is your home.'

'Not always so. Where did I live, think you, before my mother die? Before Master Piers Medley come riding along and snatch away my sister and me?'

'*Snatch away . . .?*'

'Aye – snatch and carry away.'

'Shame on you! What could've come to you, else? He took and cared for two helpless orphans – and gave you a place and let you have his name for your own. You know well you're to be his heir.'

He did not reply. His expression was set and curiously drawn, so that he looked twice his age.

'What of this home, then?' Ursula insisted. 'Tell if you must.'

'The roof's in and the walls crumbled down. There's a birch seeded in the well. Otherly, naun grow but nettles. It were the place I lived in wi' my mother and sister, where my true name got called.'

'Oh my dear man,' she cried, laughing a little, trying to bring him back to sensible matters, 'so solemn about a place you lived so little time!'

'I'll tell you why solemn – so be you swear to keep what I tell.'

'Yes, yes –'

'Swear it, then.'

'I promise. That's enough.'

He looked now as she had never seen him, very pale; almost wild. The terrible thought came to her that his strangeness, growing on him lately, was in fact some kind of sickness – madness, even . . .

'Tell me.'

'There was an old goody cared for us – Lucy and me when we were wi' our mother still . . . Goody Henty. Sister or some such to Hentys at Strives and Plashets.'

'Why, yes – I recall that. She come to our wedding.'

'After that . . . Yes, yes, I do remember; why not? After we wed, then, I never saw her more till Michaelmas of last year.'

'Well?'

The old woman had sought him out – still on her feet and hale enough, though she must be eighty years old if a day. She had brought him a plump goose for the season, saying she had wanted to see him again before she died.

'Could she not've done so any day o' the year?'

'She kept away, she said. In fear of the big house, maybe. So I could've thought – come I'd thought of her at all.'

So she had given him the goose and then had spoken of his true father.

'What did she tell, then?' Ursula asked, seeing clearly that it could not have been any pleasant recollection of past days.

'I never did know why my father died,' Robin said, speaking so low she could hardly hear, and bent towards him anxious and puzzled. 'He died a traitor's death. He died at Tyburn on a Michaelmas Day. You know what that mean?' He saw her shrink and gave her a grim little smile, cruel in itself. 'You see why my mother said naun? Too hard and bitter to be born or spoke of.'

'So the old woman told you this . . .?'

'More. She tell that he die as a traitor – but he it was who got betrayed. By one long his friend.'

Ursula did not ask who this friend might have been, for she saw already what was coming, and now she knew her husband must be mad.

'Don't say more of it,' she cried. 'You're all jawled out wi' thinking of your father . . .'

'Master Piers,' he said. 'That friend. Master Piers Medley o' Mantlemass that come, then, to ease his wicked soul by caring for the two he'd made orphans.'

Ursula's first impulse was to rush to Mantlemass, to tell Piers Medley that her husband was sick in his mind and full of dangerous and terrible thoughts. But then she was so overcome with shame at the realization of what she must say that she knew this to be impossible. So she began to seek comfort, telling herself that to learn at this late date of his father's terrible death had unhinged Robin, but that soon he would grow calmer and would then sorely repent so wild and absurd an accusation.

So she held her tongue, watching him every minute they were together, coaxing him, waiting to see that he was himself again, when she might relax her vigilance; for she felt him to be capable of disastrous behaviour. There was no way she might ease this burden – this she could not tell to Agnes, less still to her mother. She was bound to endure alone, eagerly greeting those times when he seemed his ordinary self, however brief their term. And sometimes she saw with horror how he sat long silent, seeming to be looking inward, into himself, into his own thoughts and seeing terrible things. He slept very ill, and often, waking, she found his place empty, the bed curtains thrown back; sometimes by morning he had not returned, but this was never spoken of between them.

When he was himself, then she made much of him, was fond in manner as lately she had not been, as she found it difficult to be now. Once, at such a moment, he pushed her away. A fatal and sardonic look gave him the face of a stranger.

'You demean yourself,' he said.

In this uneasy fashion the months passed and they came towards midsummer.

In her own way, Ursula too was leading two lives. In her own household she was content enough. Simon had rallied from his winter ailing and the baby, Lewis, was still fat and flourishing. But most of all she enjoyed the company of Roger Jolland, loving him not only for his own sake but for his father's whose features she traced in the younger face.

The boy had grown in every way during his stay at

Ghylls Hatch. It was almost a year and now he had turned fifteen. Country living had helped him throw back his shoulders and breathe deeper. He walked better, with a stronger, more confident step. The quiet and the stillness of the forest had calmed his manner, and no doubt his thoughts; he spoke no more of seeing and knowing. It was a wonder, too, to see the care with which Master Richard nurtured him, becoming as good as another father. His own father sent letters often, and books with them. They came to watch for his messenger, expecting always that there would be news of his own coming, as he had promised. But the books seemed to be a substitute. These young Jolland liked to read aloud to Ursula, and they opened her eyes on a magic world of 'courtoisie, poesie, amor', the precepts of chivalry that seemed to paint a thousand graceful pictures in colours both clear and delicate. She told herself that he sent the books for her, too, and though it was the son who read them, the words came to her in the father's voice.

Then at midsummer, unheralded, Sir Francis Jolland rode again to Mantlemass.

Ursula and her mother were halfway between Ghylls Hatch and Mantlemass, with Simon holding a hand of each, when young Dan Bunce came with a message from Master Piers.

'Master Piers say to fetch Sir Francis his son, madam.'

'Tell Master Piers we are all but with him, Dan.' Then she said to her mother, 'Do you go on with Simon, mother. I'll go warn Roger Jolland.'

'Warn him, daughter?'

'Aye, warn him. Sir Francis has come for his son, surelye.'

'And time enough. The boy'll be all bumpkin come he dally here longer.'

'He'll not want to go from here, that I promise. So pray keep Simon for me.'

Hearing Simon breaking instantly into wails, and Lilias's protesting, Ursula turned and ran. She was glad to turn her back. As she ran down the track, home to Ghylls Hatch, she heard herself muttering and moaning in a hopeless, helpless way: either for joy of seeing him soon, or for sadness at the thought of losing her boy, as she had called him.

Agnes was walking before the house with the baby in her arms.

'Where's my cousin, Agnes?'

'He went to the stables ... What's amiss?' asked Agnes, frowning at Ursula's strange manner and pale face.

'His father's come. Sir Francis is at Mantlemass now.'

'Lord save all,' said Agnes very low, 'do not take him that face!'

'What else may I take him?'

'Hush – be calm,' Agnes said, speaking as if to a sister. She thrust the baby into Ursula's arms. 'Take him indoors. I'll find the boy. Shall I speak of his father?'

'Best so ...'

She stood watching Agnes hurry away, not knowing where to rest her troubled thoughts.

'Tomorrow morning,' Francis Jolland had said to Ursula, as they all sat at table at Mantlemass, 'I shall visit your good mother.'

So she had gone, too, unhesitating and unashamed. Now they returned to Mantlemass together, riding slowly; then, coming to a shady place, dismounting. They stood in this solitude, far from any embrace, yet locked together heart and soul.

'You have made my boy anew,' Francis said. 'He is twice himself. I thank you for it.'

Ursula found no reply. With difficulty she looked away, knowing how much each found in the other's face, at once fearful and rejoicing, uncertain what either might say – and then, who knows, regret.

'There is much to speak of,' he said, 'and with little time for it. I see that the boy dreads returning with me.'

'Only because he loves our quiet countryside!' Ursula cried. 'Not that he loves his father any less.'

'What shall I say – or how best say it ... Since he is happiest here – shall you be happy if I leave him?'

'Oh yes! You know it! You know it well! And you shall come to visit him here ...' She broke off. 'That is – till you see fit to fetch him home.'

At this he took her hand and held it, looking down at it, then turning it palm uppermost. She wished it could be a better hand, less brown with summer, less sturdy in shape, more like a lady's, pale and helpless. 'Let it lie,' he said, as her fingers curled into a fist.

'I shall care for him as my own,' she said. 'You know how I will cherish him.'

'He is the only son I may give you, my dear heart.'

He began to speak of his own life and how it went, of his house in London, at Southwark, the garden running to the river. It was a place lived in by one Jolland and another, often re-built, garnished and freshly ornamented. He spoke of the distant marriage that had brought another Jolland to Mantlemass and so eventually made Jolland and Medley kin.

'So now I must speak what comes hardest,' Francis said at last. 'I have lost two sons – one dead, and one – wisely as I hope – passed over.'

'Then it is for ever that I have him?'

'God willing. My third son shall be heir. He is made for the world.'

Now he hesitated. They stood still with their hands touching, and he put his other hand on hers and held it very firmly.

'What remains is the worst to be said.'

She could hear the words he must speak. They came from a long way away, heavy as a trampling army. His hesitation, his pain made it necessary for her to speak first.

'You shall wed again, surelye. There must be more sons – so the inheritance is safe.'

'Yes. That is what I must tell you.'

'Choose well, then. Choose for your happiness.'

'Shall it be one who looks like you?'

'Oh no – no! As little like as may be!'

He smiled at her vehemence, and now took her hand and laid it against his heart.

'Do you feel the beat? It beats for you. It will always beat for you.'

'But be kind to her. Yes, yes – let her look like me. So, then, you shall be kind to me in loving her.'

'Poor soul. But I shall do as you bid. I shall do it.'

'Have you – are you already betrothed?'

'No.'

'But you know her name?'

'Not even that. Not yet.'

He kissed her hand and let her go, saying it was time they were on their way.

They rode slowly on through the hot summer sun of late afternoon. Then they came clear of the trees and there was Mantlemass, lying at a distance, away and a little below. The low light gilded it most marvellously, waking colour in the stone, pointing up the walls, with their crust of time, that was set layer upon layer, yet still unfinished, since time remained. As they checked their horses and paused to look across to the house, there came that sound

which Ursula knew so well, of big birds strongly winging out of a familiar distance to pass in pattern overhead.

They both gazed upward, following the flight across the brilliant sky.

'Just so they fly up river past my home,' he said. 'I always do stay a second or two for love of them.'

'Pray, then,' she said quietly, 'next when you stay for them, and for love – then think of me. Otherly, as your life goes on – shall you not altogether forget me?'

'No.'

'I shall think of you. When I pause at this hour and I see them – beautiful and strong – I shall think of you.'

'It is a pledge between us.'

'A pledge, yes.'

She touched up her horse, but he checked it, his hand on the bridle.

'Dearest Ursula – I have never heard you speak my name.'

She hesitated, uncertain and suddenly shy.

'Francis,' she said at last. Then she repeated it as once, a long time ago, she had written it, many times over.

They rode on, and reached Mantlemass.

6

Jolland

'Now,' said Jolland aloud, though for the benefit of none but his horse, 'now I am Master Jolland indeed, and a man of iron.'

The bay tossed his head obligingly; and surely every bird flying, every mouse scuttling, every deer bounding in that part of the forest must in some way have acknowledged the statement. For here was Roger Jolland, grown from that timid limping boy, with his 'seeing eye', to a young man of nineteen years, speaking with the rough tongue of a forester, and returning at this time from Plashets where he had overseen, advised, loudly rebuked and decided.

Not only Master Jolland, then, but Master Jolland of Plashets, grateful and worthy heir to Master Richard Medley who five years ago had taken the boy under his wing, instructing, cajoling, encouraging and gently bullying. So that a once reluctant pupil became a pupil who listened and looked – then not only looked but saw, not only saw but understood. He began to change, then, in manner; almost in appearance.

After perhaps three years of this progress, the head

furnaceman at Plashets had said, 'More'n half a Medley, Mus' Richard – that's what it come to.'

'But he must be called Jolland, Timothy, for he is still his father's son. Not the first time the name got spoke about these parts – his great-grandmother was a Jolland still when first she come to Mantlemass.'

It was from that day that they called him, at all times, by his father's name. He became not 'cousin Roger' but 'cousin Jolland'. With time, as names in such places as this did shift and change, he might well be known as Jolland Medley. He wore now a red cap in common with Piers and Richard Medley – as their father Master Medley had done, and even, it was claimed their grandfather. A Mantlemass man was easily spied about the forest.

He was glad of it all. It confirmed him as a person remade, a new man altogether, the conqueror of his own worst weaknesses, deeply content in the knowledge that his progress had satisfied his tutor. Richard Medley had died a little less than a twelve-month back. When that happened, then Timothy Morphew, the furnaceman, had stepped without any asking to young Master Jolland's side, never thrusting yet ever in support. And today, Jolland knew that Timothy had watched, not only in sympathy but in comfortable pride, the sternness with which the new master had rebuked a botched job, at the cold anger in which he had confronted the malingering workman. Then, before anger could cool, the Master of Plashets had swung away, mounted and ridden off quickly.

At the crossing of two tracks, Timothy Morphew was waiting.

'Mus' Jolland!'

'D'you come to tell me that were overly harsh?'

'No, master. Niver a word o' that. I come fast up the

track to meet and tell you well done! Done like any Medley, so I'd say.'

'Credit to Master Richard, then, that's gone from us.'

'Aye – rest his dear good soul. I'll swear I c'n all but hear'm rejoicing!'

The furnaceman was a one-eyed man, as many of his kind came to be, by the fierce nature of the element they worked. The eye that remained to him was bright, intelligent and very blue. He closed it in a slow wink. His dark singed face above the big beard was split into a wide grin. He stepped back and waved young Jolland on his way . . .

Jolland began to whistle softly as he rode, dropping to a contented walk, savouring the spring day. The sun had shone since early morning, but now was fast slipping to the horizon, trailing a light mist behind it. In his pleased preoccupation, the young man had passed the head of the track to Strives Minnis, and he had promised his cousin Ursula to call there on his way home, to inquire after her mother. All that last long winter through, Lilias Godman had suffered chills and agues. She had been greatly distressed by Richard Medley's death, calling it untimely, tragic, a warning to all of them that life ended all too often without any warning. He had been already in his sixties, and she must surely have twenty years still left to her if she lived as long, but her melancholy had persisted. She stayed more and more at home, with only Nance Tester to care for her. Indeed the prospect of a visit did not greatly enthrall Jolland, and maybe that was why he had passed the turning before his conscience tweaked at Pilgrim's rein. Lilias's sharp manner had scared Jolland when he first came to the forest, and he was still a little in awe of her – though maybe less so now that he shared with her the precious mastership of iron.

Dutifully, unwilling to disappoint his cousin, Jolland pulled Pilgrim's head round. As he did so there was a swift, sharp movement among the birch scrub and gorse over his right shoulder. The movement of deer about the forest made such rustling movements common enough, though it was early in the day for deer to be abroad in that more frequented part. He went on his way without considering too much about it, and had forgotten the incident by the time he reached Strives.

The place by now had grown very shabby. It had the air of sadness that hangs always about a derelict working, as if the labour poured out over the years had been in vain. The ground was dusty, bald even of weed, dead. Mounds of cinder and of ash seemed to signify too much of life and its changes. A few hens pecked among the spoil of worked-out stone about the house and along the track that led off to the emptied pond.

Nance Tester was about to shut up the hens, and she waited for the rider to approach. Her son Peter, a lear and uncouth man in his thirties, with less to his wits than most, came to take Pilgrim's bridle.

'Tether him – I'll not be long indoors . . . How's your mistress, goody?' Jolland asked Nance.

'A shade partic'ler. Eats little and sleeps less.'

'Better she come to Mantlemass,' he said. 'How many long year since her daughter urge her to that?'

'She will not. There's naun she need but what she find here. Her own place – not any other's. Besides –'

Nance broke off, a bit red in the face. He knew very well what she meant, an old servant who doubtless knew more about the Medleys than the Medleys knew themselves. Lilias made no secret of finding herself less and less able to tolerate her daughter's husband. Jolland would have liked to say 'He's not much at home', but could not go quite so far in confidence with someone's else's servant, trusted or not. Indeed he had never been altogether certain that Nance was so utterly trustworthy. He thought she probably did well for herself and her unprepossessing son; if Lilias came to Mantlemass, things might not go so easily for Nance. Once, he had said as much to Ursula, but she had known Nance so long she hardly saw what she looked at, and she brushed the idea aside.

'I'll speak with her, Nance,' Jolland said.

He had not seen Lilias since Christmastide. Even had the weather been less fierce, she had not been well enough to be out and about. The severe winter had kept them all mewed up, every forest man and woman, on their own land, large or small. So, when he went indoors and found Lilias on the settle by the hearth, a shawl over her shoulders, another on her knees, he was shocked by the change in her.

'I'm come for news of you,' he said, 'sent here by your own good daughter.' And for the first time ever, he addressed her by that form which she had won for herself in her working days. 'My cousin Ursula fret after you, master.'

She looked up at him sharply. 'Master? You niver did call me master till this day.'

'This day,' he said, savouring the words, 'I am Master, too. Master Jolland o' Plashets.'

Now Lilias smiled. Not her usual brief, grudging smile, but one touched with warmth, almost with excitement.

'Why, then,' she said, 'see you stay strong like iron, in your own body, and in your mind. I know what I say. To them that sees it, iron is all.'

'See you watch me, master, and keep me to it!'

She was looking at him now in the deepest consideration.

'Who could've thought you'd ever come so well out o' that childhood of yourn, Roger Jolland.'

'I'm new forged,' he told her. 'Master Richard say so. And t'were him did the forging.'

'What of your father? Seeing you so set-up and sprackish – shall he not carry you back to his world?'

'I'd not seem sprackish there!' He laughed to consider what his father might think of the outlandish word.

'But he's not forgot you, Master Jolland o' Plashets.'

It was true. His father might be said to have given him away – and not the first parent to act so. But he had written at least three times in every year, and sent books with each letter. And when he took his second wife he sent his son her painted likeness. Young Jolland had stood with it in the palm of his hand, and had looked up at Ursula, crying out in amazement, 'Save the colour of her hair, her picture might be yours!' And he held it out to her. 'Look, cousin, look!'

'Keep it for yourself,' she had said, her voice low. And she had walked away . . .

'I think of my father often, as I know he think of me,' he told Lilias. 'But he'd have no place for a foresty fellow at his side – that I do know and understand well.'

'Well, you seem my daughter's boy now. Best I settle to another grandson, then.'

Impulsively, easy with her as never before, he put his arm around her shoulder and kissed her cheek. He felt how she pulled away, yet knew she was not angry.

'Master Grandmother!' he cried.

At that she laughed loudly and with pleasure. But then she started coughing, and went into a paroxysm she could not control. He feared she might choke, and shouted for Nance. It was as if she had been waiting, for she came with a draught already mixed and held it for Lilias to drink. Then Lilias was quiet, but lay back on the settle exhausted, her eyes closed.

'You must take care,' Jolland said.

'Ah – surelye ...' she answered her voice curiously slurred.

'Best leave her,' Nance said.

He frowned. 'She look so strange and dwiney, Nance.' And again he said to Lilias, shaking her arm, 'Your daughter say to take care for her sake.'

This time Lilias did not attempt to reply. Her head lolled and her eyes were all but closed, though showing the whites a little at the rim in an almost deathlike manner.

'What come to her?' he cried.

'The draught make her drowsy.'

'So quickly? What strong stuff is that you give her?'

'Her own brewing.' Nance answered him sulkily, and though he pressed her to say more, she would only mutter about Lilias being better in bed and she'd be sure to see her settled in.

At last, defeated, he left the house and rode away. He frowned as he went, thinking for the first time of the two women alone day by day at Strives. The strange thought slid into his mind that Lilias could be Nance's prisoner ...

The spring day had chilled as the dusk began. The forest stirred now to the start of its night time business. Now the deer were moving freely, and he reined in and waited to watch a doe cross the track with a fawn at her heel, a yearling, almost, and lame, so that it hesitated and tottered behind its mother. Jolland watched smiling. His country cousins had taught him a softness for all animals.

Jolland shook up Pilgrim and moved on his way quietly. Strives land melted without any boundary into the forest.

It was no more than a small parcel with a good supply of water and, until a few years ago, rich ore for the taking. The place had seen many changes. Now came the latest, maybe the last, as it began to be re-absorbed into the forest, eventually to be hidden and all but consumed by scrub that grew and thickened at almost magical speed.

Pilgrim started and snorted, stepping sharply sideways, so that Jolland, so lazily musing, was all but shaken out of the saddle. He knew that there had been once more that quick movement in the underwood. This time it surely must be deer – yet as he told himself it was so, and rode on firmly, Jolland found himself uneasy almost to the point of alarm. There was something – there was something more than the usual movement, the breaking of twigs, the rustle of leaves, the swaying of branches thrust aside, the alarm cry of a bird put up violently, shrieking as it flew.

As he came by the head of a track that looped back towards Strives, he saw a man walking rapidly away from him. Instinctively, the rider checked, slipping behind birches alongside his road.

Though he was turned away and walking swiftly, Jolland knew the man to be a stranger. There was something more than hasty about him, a certain furtiveness that claimed attention; had Pilgrim been more than strolling so alert a walker must have heard him and turned. Well, there were many who moved through the forest with their ears pricked, using the place for shelter and concealment and rest – rogues and cheap scoundrels of one kind or another, with sometimes a gentleman or two in flight because of politics or religion. It would not have occurred to Jolland to hail any such, but he waited, indefinably uneasy, looking after the stranger until he had vanished, noting the cut of his jerkin, the colour of his hair

beneath a dark russet cap pulled low.

'Best leave him about his business,' he muttered at last to Pilgrim.

Then he moved on his way.

When Richard Medley died, the family at Ghylls Hatch had moved to Mantlemass for the comfort and care of Master Piers. But Robin Medley had never settled there. He came and went, now staying with the horses at Ghylls Hatch, now going about his own particular concerns, which no one had ever fathomed or surprised him into naming. Over the years he had time and again traded the horses as Master Piers did not approve, and there had often been most bitter conflict between the two. Now it was as if the older man had shrugged his shoulders and turned away.

Once he had said, 'He is his father's son, not mine. How else should he be at his father's age?'

At Mantlemass, on the first day of this year, Ursula had given birth to a son who seemed likely to be her last child. Everyone knew, without speaking of it, that from the first night after their removal to Mantlemass she slept with her door barred. So now there was Jolland's godson, called always by his second name, Lewis; a daughter, Susan, now two years old, and Thomas, the baby. She had lost three and kept three, which was at once more and less than many women of her age and condition could claim. The last two children seemed bounding and fine, but Jolland had little hope for his godson's future. The summer fever that had killed Simon had destroyed, too, all Lewis's early promise.

Coming up the last bank towards Mantlemass, he saw Ursula at the door – looking out for him, perhaps, to hear news of her mother. There was some light indoors and she stood with her shadow thrown ahead of her. One of the children ran from the house and clasped her about the knees – the two-year-old Susan, with Agnes Goodale chasing after her. Jolland saw rather than heard their laughter as Ursula swung her skirts and the little girl darted to hide behind them, while Agnes, clapping her hand, swooped here and there, this side and that, making much of being unable to catch her. Then he was near enough to hear, too. The laughter splintering merrily over the dusky trees below, scattering beneath the darkening sky, moved him to a feeling of comfort and homecoming.

Agnes scooped up the child, swinging her round and carrying her indoors, with Ursula following.

But at the threshold, Ursula paused and looked back, her head raised, listening.

Jolland smiled at this familiar picture of his cousin. For she would stand just so at this hour of the day, often and often, waiting for the sound of the swans returning from the marshes to their own place by the far ponds. This evening and for some time there would be fewer, for many had nested and bred and only the young cobs were free to make the daily journey.

He waved and shouted, and Ursula saw him and waved back. He cantered to the house.

'How is my mother?' she would ask.

And he would tease her by telling of his 'master grandmother'. 'But she look a shade more'n sickly,' he would be bound to say. 'Nance brought some drink that soothed her . . .' He would not at that time say more.

'Jolland found my mother a shade low, sir,' Ursula Medley said to Master Piers as they sat at supper.

Piers frowned. He had been low himself through that winter, missing his brother, full of trouble over Robin

Medley's behaviour, and the way that marriage had gone that once had been so full of delight.

'Speak to her again about quitting Strives,' he said. 'She'll hear naun from me – but do you try yet again, daughter. What life is that she lives, no company but servants' company, and the place set to crumble about her ears.'

'I'll go to her tomorrow,' Ursula promised. 'But I doubt I'll get a hearing.' Then glancing towards the door she said without any change of tone, 'There now. My husband see fit to come for his supper.'

The last few years had changed Robin Medley. He had coarsened; broadened at the shoulder, thickened at the waist. He was thirty years old, no more, but his face, toughened by weather, was prematurely lined; there was grey in his hair. His expression had become curiously secret, and just as he lived for the greater part physically removed from the rest of them, so too his mind was shut away. Briefly and without warning there might flash out even now some remnant of his younger self; because of it, Ursula had remained loyal to her marriage long past the point of endurance. But Jolland had seen Robin looking at Master Piers, who had given him all it lay in any man's power to give – a name, a living, a truly parental love – with a reserve so near to hatred that it was frightening.

Although Jolland was presumed to have got over, grown out of – whatever phrase his elders chose to employ; exorcized would have been more apt – the seeing eye that had troubled his childhood, he knew that it persisted. Not only in such vague unease as had stirred him twice today, but in a perception of character that was at times like looking through the eyes of a man into his soul. He had often thought that more doors than one should be barred against Robin Medley.

Now, as he took his place at table, Robin made no more than a mumbled apology, falling to at once on the dishes set before him.

'You've been unseen, these three days'n more,' Piers said. 'What business kept you?'

'Tom Awcock took sick. I went searching out a farrier.'

'Not far to search, I'd think.'

'I went after young Tester, that's nephew to Awcock – his sister's son – lives a mile this side town.'

'And did you bring him back?'

'He'd half the gentry at his door.'

'What then?'

'Come I reached home agin, Awcock was well and the need gone.'

Piers did not reply to this, for there seemed, indeed, very little to say. He poured himself more wine, his hand shaking slightly. He was now too old to struggle with Robin, but too old to be patient with him, either. Jolland watched him with a deep and tender pity, knowing he must die soon, and all the long years of his vigour, of his heartbreaks and his humour would be lost and forgotten. What would this place be without him? It had been bad enough when Richard Medley went, but when Master Piers left Mantlemass then surely one whole world must end ...

'What was your day, cousin Jolland?' Piers asked, turning with an appearance of irritated relief to the younger man.

'There was some little trouble at Plashets, sir. Downstream at the forge, that is. A set o' skillets done for the farmhouse – the whole bodged and shapeless.'

'Maybe that work seem altogether niggling and solly to Plashets men. It's guns they handle best.'

'They need settle for skillets and such,' said Ursula. 'War's done with.'

'So my brother Richard might've said – but not your mother! Let be how't will – the order's out we should give over forging arms. What wisdom or folly's in that – we'll know one day.'

Jolland wished to change the subject. He had been pleased with himself for his day's work but he felt the need to cheer Master Piers away from everyday matters.

'There was some stranger in our forest today,' he said.

He saw Robin lift his head from his platter, flick a glance towards the head of the table, then get back to his victuals.

'Well,' Piers answered, 'we cannot know the name of all who choose this way from one place to the next.'

'I'd think him a hiding man, sir.'

'But not hid deep enough, it seem!'

'Maybe you saw some Sackville spy, come searching out poachers,' Robin Medley said. 'There's a mortacious lot o' deer bin taken, these last years.'

'They'll take freer from the Master of Game than from the Crown,' Piers said, chuckling a little. 'The penalty's the same, but the sport's better.'

Some years ago, the Queen had made Sir Richard Sackville master of the forest and its game. Since then, Piers had often told Jolland, the running battle between the foresters and authority had been sharper and fiercer than ever before. He made this pronouncement with all the conviction of an old man come to believe he had been alive since the beginning of time.

'And this,' he remarked, turning the meat before him, 'is a very fine bit of venison we are now eating. Well hung, well cooked, and I doubt not well shot. Whose hand, I do wonder, sped that bolt? Did your stranger carry a weapon, cousin?'

'What quality of man?' Ursula asked. 'You said little of him yet.'

'Of good quality. Wearing cloth well cut . . .'

He broke off, thinking how little time he had had to judge such matters, curiously startled by the positive tone he had used, the certainty of his words. He found himself chasing a thought against talk that now broke out, following some remark of Robin's, about Ghylls Hatch matters. He could not quite name what he was seeking round the back and corners of his mind. It was there – then it was gone. Almost, it fled because he willed it so, uncertain if he wanted to know its name and purpose.

He began to sweat uncomfortably, and would have pulled at the neck of his doublet only he feared to attract attention.

Even so, Ursula asked him was he well?

'The meat was well spiced. It burnt my throat . . .'

Only many hours later, waking from a terrifying and enveloping dream, the sweat this time pouring, was he startled into naming his thought.

7

A Stranger

At cock-crow, Jolland fell into his first deep sleep of the long night, and slept on as the house began to stir. When he awoke, it was to a feeling of panic, of urgency so extreme that he leapt from his bed and began to drag and fumble at his clothes, missing eyelets and all but pulling his right sleeve over his left arm. He was filled with self-disgust. What Master Richard had called his 'weakness' and urged him to conquer was not tamed at all – it had been waiting, all these years, coiled and cunning and ready to spring. This was no mere niggle of apprehension, such as he had learnt how to dismiss. It was the full terrifying force of seeing as he had been used to see – and none of it promising any better than those events he had known so clearly in the past – his own mother's death, his brother's loss.

Struggling with his jerkin, Jolland ran down the wide stairway that had been Master Medley's pride, that still made Mantlemass grand beyond its situation.

The maids were at work in the hall, sprinkling the rushes that were dusty with winter and must be renewed for Easter. Since Ursula returned to Mantlemass all was indeed 'sprugged-up'. Almost the first thing she had done was to sweep out the rushes with cries of disgust. New had been strewn on old three and four times and she swore there were rats nesting in the gubber along with great hordes of mice.

The door was standing open to the spring morning, sunny, sharp and clean. The day seemed to have started long ago. Milking was done, and the two or three cows kept through the winter for the house had been returned to pasture. Little for them to graze, and both hay and straw low at this season. Days of marketing lay ahead; they would buy young cattle from the drovers coming through from the west, when they skirted the deep forest, watering at the farm up on the crossing of the old road, where the three yew trees stood.

Such matters, plain day-to-day labouring, blunted a little the ragged edge of Jolland's anxiety.

Agnes Goodale, coming indoors with an armful of linen left out overnight for bleaching, called a greeting. Then she paused and looked more nearly at him, frowning slightly.

'Are you well, sir?'

'Yes – yes . . . Where is Dame Ursula?'

'She took the children to the pond. There's two clutch o'duckling, early hatched.'

'I'll find her . . .'

He went out of the house, glad of the sharpness on the air that cleared his brain a little. But it was walking along this very courtyard that he had listened to Master Richard urging him to be rid of the childish folly of foreboding and forseeing. The last years of change seemed then to be scattered like leaves across the forest.

Ursula was beside the pond with Lewis and Susan. The boy leant against his mother, languid and thin, but Susan ran and skipped, then stood at the water's edge with her fists bunched against her cheeks and her shoulders hunched with excitement, as the mother duck swam fast and faster, side to side and up and down, the chicks drawn behind her as if on invisible threads.

Three times, as Jolland approached, one of the men from the farm paused to watch, and then went on his way laughing. It was a scene so innocent that Jolland checked and the temper of the moment changed for him. Surely he had had a bad dream and that was all the sum of it? He slowed his pace, attempting to order his thoughts and to control his manner. What had he to tell Ursula that could make any kind of good sense? Had he indeed the boldness to tell her that in the dark sweating moment past midnight, he had known beyond any doubt that his brother was returned?

She looked up as he came near and called out to him.

'A fine morning, cousin – so bless us all! Come here – and see what we see.' Then as he reached her side, she frowned as Agnes had done. 'Are you well?'

'Do I look otherly?'

'Aye – peaked and dwindled. What ails you?'

He felt his hands shaking and clenched them behind his back. For good or ill he had to tell her what he had seen and not seen.

'Let me speak with you.'

She looked about her. A girl carrying pails on a yoke was passing the pond.

'Come here, Mary, and watch the ducklings – but mind you do also watch the children.'

Mary set down the pails. The children ran to grab her hands. Ursula turned to Jolland ... Seconds only before he must find words for what he had to say.

'It is a confidence,' he began.

'I'm no nabbler, Jolland.' She looked at him with concern and he would not meet her eyes. 'Shall we go into the house?' she asked.

'Aye, come you wish. No – we are alone here.'

'Tell me . . .'

He took a breath that whistled through his teeth, as if at some sharp unavoidable pain.

'I have seen my brother.'

For a second there was a great radiance in her face, but gone as soon as glimpsed.

'Your *brother*? I thought you said . . .' She had now lost her colour a little. 'What *brother*?' she asked flatly.

'Humfrey. Humfrey Jolland.'

'Now what folly?' she cried, sharply irritated. 'You mean that you saw a stranger yesterday. Aye, you told that last evening. So you have let yourself get to dreaming all the hours since and here's all this old nonsense to do again. Humfrey Jolland is dead these long years and well you know it. As do we all,' she insisted, her voice rising, 'else why should your – your father been set to – to wed again and get more sons?'

'In my heart – I knew he'd not died.'

'Oh for certain – you were forever seeing this and promising that! But you were a child, then, and what you must see now is only truth. Your brother is gone. Humfrey Jolland is dead. The sea has him. He shall not be thought of again, save to mourn. He shall not be thought of by any one of us!'

He could not understand her manner. Her eyes had filled with tears, and he had hardly seen such a thing before. She was always firm and certain, or so it seemed. She had never, to his knowledge, needed tears as some women might to make a point, unless she were in low health. He had known her weep a long while ago at the time his godson was born – but that had been another matter. When young Simon sickened and died so fast, just short of his fifth birthday, she had stayed strong and stony and rigidly quiet. Indeed it was then he had heard her say, though he had not altogether understood, that tears belonged to the past . . .

'Why do you speak so plain and foreright?' he asked. 'You never did say a cruel word to me ever till this.'

'Not cruel. Truthful. For all our sakes – for your father who trusted you here – you must give up these fancies!'

They stood in the increasing sunshine. The children stayed by the pond. Mary laughed with Susan, and once even Lewis raised a little shout. The day's doings increased. Three riders passed below on the track beyond the Mantlemass pale, and called a greeting as they went. A man on foot approached from the direction of Ghylls Hatch. Agnes came again from the house, this time with the baby, Thomas, in her arms. There was a sound of hammering somewhere out of sight, and the heavy thud of some greater hammer away at a neighbouring foundry. And there was a huge and boisterous sound of birdsong. The familiar surge of forest noises, uncounted, unnamed, filled the morning with a growing purpose and intent. With every crowded second, the season advanced.

'Well,' Jolland said, defeated, 'I see I'd better not've spoke.'

Before she could answer, there was a great shout from the doorway of the house. Master Piers stood there, calling, waving and beckoning. It was amazing what a voice he could raise out of himself when he chose, whatever his years.

'Here! Here to me! Ursula! Jolland! News!'

Jolland paused long enough to see Ursula's colour change again, from pale, this time, to red.

'Shall it be my stranger?' he said.

She turned and went swiftly towards the house, and he followed.

Master Piers was smiling. He held out his hand to Ursula and drew her indoors, calling to Jolland to follow.

Had his father come? Had his brother come from hiding . . .?

There was a man standing in the hall. Not his father. Not his brother. A stranger.

'A traveller,' Piers said. 'Journeyed far. Seeks work, so he tell. I never let'm speak a word more till you're with me. He tell me he's been in Dean forest!'

'Is it truly news, then, sir?' Ursula said. 'Of Harry Medley? Of *your* brother?'

'I've asked naun till you come – we'll hear together what he have to tell. Where're you from, I asked him. And when he answer – then I come straight bawling for you and cousin Jolland!'

The stranger, who was most certainly not Jolland's stranger, was a short dark man, square and strong. He held his cap in his hand and worked it round and round as if it were a platter to be dried. His eyes, small and bright, looked from Ursula to Piers, to Jolland and back again. It was a curious, flickering look, half engaging, half shifty; it matched his rather uneasy smile. He seemed to Jolland to be a man surprised and uncertain how to deal with his surprise.

'You were about the forest yesterday, were you?' Piers asked him.

'Seeking my way, you see, sir. Learning, since it was iron founding I came to seek, how I was best to find out Master Piers Medley at Mantlemass.' He gave another quick glance from one to the other. 'As I have.'

'There, cousin,' Piers said. 'There's your stranger!' He gave that quick laugh that took the years off his shoulders as if by magic. 'Now – let's speak of Harry Medley.'

Jolland was concerned at that moment most with the fact that this was certainly not the man he had seen yesterday. What this fellow might have to tell of Master Medley's eldest son, so long gone from Mantlemass, could have little interest for Jolland. It was not Piers Medley's brother that he wished to hear spoken of.

'So now,' Piers was saying, 'you came from Dean forest. And so you can tell me of Master Harry Medley. And of his sons? Jack was the eldest, and Lewis next.'

The man said slowly, 'I do know that forest, sir.'

'His dwelling is there. That I am certain of. A fellow came once before from those parts. Prosperous, so he say. Rich and prosperous.'

'There's strange, now,' said the man.

'Wait!' Piers took up a jug of wine that stood on the side board alongside a range of old drinking cups. 'Sit down. Let this be friendly. Drink, friend, and tell your tale.'

The man's unease was now apparent, though he strove to conceal it. Also there was a dawning of something near contempt, for this was a strange way to be greeted by such a man as Piers Medley, master of a fine house, and little dignity in it, he seemed to suggest – but he was willing to humour an old man.

Jolland glanced at Ursula and saw her frown.

'Is it so?' she asked. 'Are you from Dean?'

'It is aye and it is nay, mistress,' he answered, his voice with its singing tone very clear and precise. 'I am from further, look you; from near Caernarvon. I have skirted the forest on my travels here, I know its men – miners and such. This has been my work, I can tell you – you will see its mark in my complexion.'

Sure enough, he had that singed, ruddy-brown look that was so familiar, his skin pitted as if it had been nicked by flying fragments of stone. But most of all his face suggested that he was at a loss, at a disadvantage – as if, expecting to answer one set of questions he found himself faced with others and was not primed.

'Now,' Piers said, turning from the board and handing the full cup. 'Sit down – sit down! Tell all you know. But first let's have your name.'

'Watkyn,' he answered, short and firm.

'Then, Watkyn, give us your news. Master Harry Medley, now – a man of iron in the great forest of Dean.'

At this Watkyn's face cleared slightly, as if he had been offered some clue he needed. He sat down gingerly on the stool Piers had shoved towards him.

'Sir,' he said carefully, 'it is not, see you, that I exactly know your brother . . .'

Piers frowned. The elation died and he said almost petulantly, 'You told me you'd bin his man and worked for'm.'

'No, no – I did not. I – I did *hear* of such a master of iron – that was it! And why else, in these parts, do I seek you, sir? There's something, then! I am told to seek work from *you*!'

Ursula was standing behind Piers as he sat bending anxiously towards Watkyn. She put her hands on his shoulders and stooped down to him, speaking fondly and gently.

'Let the fellow tell what he know, sir, though it be little. Seems me your brother must be alive and well.'

Watkyn shifted slightly, looking from one to the other. He seemed to decide what he must say. 'Hard it is to tell, mistress – but it was no Master Harry I heard of. It was – it was Master Lewis! Yes – that was it. Master Lewis

Medley.' He seemed to get into his stride, then, and the details rattled out. 'A solid man, indeed. Upward of forty years, I would say. Handsome. His lady very beautiful ...'

Piers sat silent, staring at him, still frowning.

'Is it so?' he said at last, very quietly. 'Ah – yes, I see. I have quite missed out the many years since – since we lost him.' He put his hand and pressed Ursula's, which still rested on his shoulder. 'Lewis was the baby when they left,' he said. He made a sad grimace. 'So Harry's dead. Poor Harry. He did seem too strong for any but himself. I never thought of him ailing or dying ... And then there was Jack – Jack was his eldest. Did you hear nothing of him?'

Watkyn shook his head rather vaguely – and then at once with firmness, saying, 'No. No. No word.'

'Let this be a lesson to me, then. I think too little of passing time. My brother Richard had said some such thing of me once.'

He rose, then, his wine untasted. With a brief nod at the Welshman, who had jumped to his feet, he went slowly across the hall and out of the open door into the spring sunshine.

'Best I be gone, then,' Watkyn said; but with a query in his voice. 'It was work I wanted.'

Jolland knew that Ursula was looking to him now and that he must be Master Jolland of Plashets. It was for him to decide what should be done about the stranger.

'You are a foreigner,' he said. 'They're unkindly thought of, most often, in these parts. You'd be bound to take your chance with the rest.'

'Oh I would do that gladly, sir – gladly!'

'You made a mortacious long journey, seems me. Was there no work in other places?'

'Not for me,' said Watkyn.

There was the least hint of insolence in his tone, and Jolland knew that Ursula heard it, too. He knew also that she was watching him, not only with encouragement but with a kind of confident pride. And after all, had she not often and often claimed him as her boy, her eldest, her first son Roger for whom a later had been named; and entrusted to her by his father? Perhaps, too, she watched him as Master Richard's pupil, waiting to learn how much he had inherited of wisdom, experience and strength . . .

'Which trade do you ply?'

'I am a smith, master.'

'Show me your hands.'

Perceptibly, the man recoiled. In a strangely childish fashion he slid his hands behind his back, then wiped them down his thighs.

'I have my full ten fingers, look you.'

'How shall I know that, since you keep them hid?' A certain masterly amusement in Jolland's tone would be hard for any but a snivelling fellow to swallow meekly. He smiled slightly to temper his own harshness – and then the man did hold out one hand palm uppermost, a grudging compromise that saved him a little dignity.

It was a good strong hand, short-fingered, broad-palmed with a hefty wrist. But it was clean – too clean by far.

'Many a long day since that hand took up hammer or pincers, I'd say.' Jolland glanced at Ursula and she came beside him and looked in turn at Watkyn's hand. He snatched it to his side, clenching it into a fist. Jolland shrugged. 'All but a townsman's paw,' he said.

For a second Watkyn hesitated. Now that flickering glance was seen as shifty and vengeful. He looked from one to the other, rammed his hat discourteously on his head, dragging it down to his ears. Saying curtly, 'Good

day to you,' he marched across the floor and out into the air.

'Where'll he go now?' Jolland wondered. 'And why should he ever come?'

'Men do so wander, never settling. We see 'em enough in these parts, the dear Lord knows.'

'Maybe. But I do wonder, cousin, that he knew so much – and yet so little.'

'He saw his advantage, maybe. Let be how't will – at the least you know now who it was you saw yesterday.'

'It was another I saw, cousin.'

'Oh do be done with pathery, childish nonsense!' she cried impatiently. 'I saw you could not help it once – but it is cured and done with!'

'It come again, like a fever. Can I help it? I see now it's part of my nature and must be endured. Like my leg that's got its little twist.'

'You fought that!'

'Aye – and won a bit. But who's to tell if it stay so?'

'Let be,' Ursula said then. 'We are all but quarrelling. We never should do so – and never have.'

At once, very gladly, he put his arms about her and kissed her cheek. He had grown tallish in the last eight years; he must by now be much about his father's height. He remembered noticing how small Ursula looked beside his father, and so he found her now, but without one jot of weakness.

'You're my second mother, these years,' he said. 'How should we quarrel, then? Forgive me. I am being a bad son.'

'No, no – truly ... We both need what we may not have and that put us in a fluster.'

She spoke in a low sad voice that he had not heard

before. Then as if to cover her words she said that Master Piers, too, shared their state. 'You want to know your brother lives – so does he wish for Harry Medley. While I – well, truly, I have no brother to mourn.'

He supposed she spoke of her husband and the sorrow he had brought her. Or did she mean differently? Had she, perhaps, some other image she yearned after? And again, his mind's eye showed her standing at his father's side . . .

'Best be about your work, Jolland,' she said, 'and I'll get to mine. Else I'll find Mary's ducked the children in the pond for very weariness of waiting on me!'

It seemed likely to be a day of irritations. When he went to the stables for his horse he found young Dick Ade who worked there fussing about with poultices.

'His pastern swell, master. See it – here? That look like some thorn or such fester. He'll never be rid this two-three days to come.'

'Saddle me Iris, then.'

'Master Piers took Iris, half an hour gone.'

'Where to?'

'Ghylls Hatch, sir. There was old and young Bunce come up bawling after'm, and they talked and he goo off wi'm.'

Jolland looked round the stables and realized suddenly that they had grown scant of horses, the last twelvemonth. Ghylls Hatch and Mantlemass made up the sum of riding animals in that corner of the forest – years ago a Master of the Game had tried to curtail their privileges in this respect, but without any great success. By now, Medleys were born stubborn as any other in the Weald.

'What come to Diana and old Topaz?' he asked.

'Why, sir, they was all took down to Ghylls Hatch, two-three month or so past.'

'And Drummer?' Jolland asked, naming the ugly old black Piers had taken to after the death of Agon.

'Drummer, too, Mus' Jolland.'

For a moment Jolland was, as they said, nonplush. Then he said, grinning at the lad, that his own two hoofs should carry him for a change.

'Horses, horses! It's forever horses does the hard work. Watch me and see how well I do without 'em!'

The boy laughed very willingly. There was respect and plain liking in his face – the last of however many Ades to work in these stables? There would be no more till he got some sons of his own, for the family had dwindled to sisters. Dwindled had been their father's dismissive word, but the sisters were a sprightly, clever lot – the second of them, Joan, had come lately to work in the house with Agnes Goodale.

As he walked off down the steep bank, Jolland knew that young Dick was watching him. At once he became conscious of that slight lameness he had all but beaten by learning a clever stride. It added to his general feeling of unease, almost of confusion. He began to tell himself that Ursula might have been right, and that the stranger he had seen was none other than Watkyn. He felt diminished by her flare of impatience and sought some way by which he could placate her.

The day, after its bright beginning, had clouded. As he went across that open part of the forest that had once been thickly grown with birch and alder, he felt rain on his face. He turned off into woodier parts as soon as he was able, and before long found himself at the mouth of that track where yesterday he had watched his stranger. It was as good a way as any once some shelter became welcome, though it wound round by Strives Minnis and only then by a little-trodden way to Plashets. The going all the way was rough and to his annoyance Jolland began to feel the weakness in his ankle. The thought of returning home on foot, when his work was done, was not inviting. He would have been more sensible to wait while Dick fetched him a horse from Ghylls Hatch, and might have done so if the day until then had not been so full of confusion. Because of it, he had forgotten to break his fast – but he would make a virtue of this and stop at Strives to beg bread and ale and see how Lilias Godman fared.

Thus he excused himself for taking this way, knowing well in his heart why he had in fact chosen to do so. A man once seen on any given track was very likely to be seen there again – a way once learned became an anchor and a starting point for any stranger.

The track to Strives, that had been well worn when the furnace was blowing, had quickly lost its urgent air. Such ways did very quickly change, and with little time would close right over and be forgotten with the rest. Already brambles leant in from either side ready to meet and clasp, and what had been beaten ground had grown rutty and covered with tufts of coarse grass. It was very quiet. Though birds must be busy in the higher branches they made no noise about it, and there was no scurry today among the underwood. Rain pattered on branches only budding, then steadied and fell on the head and shoulders of the walker.

He came to Strives and Lilias was standing at the door, looking out over the forest as he had often seen her. She was more herself than she had appeared yesterday, and once again he wondered if his imagination had been playing pranks.

'I niver saw you afoot since you were so high,' she said, sounding her roughest. 'I scarce knew you – I thought you some misagift stranger.'

'Do you see so many?' he asked quickly.

'More'n you see at Mantlemass, could be. It's deep here and a place for hiding.'

'Who's hid, then, these last times?'

'None I could name. Strangers are not for naming, Mus' Jolland o' Plashets. Come they're named, what's strange to be seen in 'em?'

'But you've seen someone nameless – yesterday? The day afore that?'

'Maybe yes, maybe no. Ask Nance. Her sight's sharper'n mine's fast growing.'

She went into the house, pushing him ahead of her, then pulling his wet cloak from his shoulders and shaking it.

'Nance! Nance! Come here when I need!'

Nance appeared slowly, pointedly wiping her hands on her apron, frowning slightly.

'Nance, Master Jolland's not broke his fast. Set him a collation and quick about it. And, Nance –'

'Aye? What else?'

'Was it yesterday that fellow passed?'

'What fellow?'

'Him that tore his cap on the low branch at the gate – the oak branch, woman.'

'I misremember. Who tore his cap?'

'Why, he did – and you laughed at it.'

'One o' your dreams,' Nance said, turning back to the kitchen.

'Yesterday, Master Grandmother? Was it yesterday?'

'One day's like another. Maybe. Maybe not.'

Jolland got no more from Lilias. After eating and drinking, he said goodbye and went on his way.

As he passed under the low-branched oak alongside a hanging gate that had once guarded a strip of pasture,

Jolland glanced up curiously. As he did so, a mistle thrush flew off with something in its beak. It could easily have been a shred of cloth, a find for a nesting bird. The idea was so fanciful that it broke his mood by making him laugh. He glanced again at the oak's low branch and saw there precisely the sort of protruding twig that might hook a man's cap from his head and keep it hanging before he could snatch it – maybe leaving a shred or two behind. No shred was to be seen now, however, and whether the thrush was to blame Jolland could never know.

The rest at Strives had restored him, certainly in body, even a little in spirit. He swung on his way, facing now down a track he had never before used. But he had developed over the years a forester's instinct for direction; he had no doubt that this was the track that would eventually lead him near Plashets.

This was a much smaller path, little more than a deer run, but it had clearly been used lately by someone needing wider berth. Here there was undergrowth thrust back, the occasional broken trailer of honeysuckle, trampled primroses.

The track wound very deep among the trees, the ground falling away into a hollow so steep-sided it might almost be called a ravine. It was a stiff scramble up the far side. A fair outcropping of stone, the way the ground humped, gave Jolland the impression that at any moment he could be staring into the mouth of a cave. This must surely be the site of some ancient mine, long discarded and forgotten. There was a slight watery sound. Many ferns grew along the margin of a bright green bog, their new fronds throwing up the first furred coils among the wilting fans of last year. He was glad to reach higher ground, the hollow seemed to him strangely haunted, even threatening. Once free of it he found the ground opening out, the trees standing back obediently. A clearing lay ahead, and one freshly trimmed, for many small trees lay stacked. By whom? For whom?

He was answered almost immediately. As he reached the clearing he saw that it contained a dwelling, small but sturdy, more than a hovel but less than a house. It looked newly built, or at least newly set to rights, for the roof thatch was clean and the walls unmossed. Smoke rose from the chimney and as Jolland drew near a man came from the open door. He carried a hatchet and a sack and went purposefully across to the woodpile and began selecting what he needed. The wood he chose was already cut into useable lengths. He set them on end, swung his axe, and skilfully and neatly split them in two.

He gathered the wood into the sack, lifted it on his shoulder, and made for the house door. As if attracted by some sound, he looked directly towards Jolland, who had moved quickly between two concealing trunks.

He was dark, neatly bearded, young, and utterly familiar. He was yesterday's stranger but much more.

He was Humfrey Jolland, as his brother had known he must be.

8

Trouble

For a second, the world seemed suspended, time to cease.

Unseeing, Humfrey turned and carted his wood indoors. The door thudded behind him. Did he speak? Had there been voices within the house? Jolland was too confused to be sure. As soon as the door closed he sank down on the wet ground. He felt exhausted, as though he had travelled far and returned worn out. There was no joy in what he had seen, only threats that he hardly dared give shape. Nothing could have given him means to spring forward and challenge Humfrey – long lost, miraculously restored, returned in health and strength though utterly changed. Who could ever have supposed that 'stomachy lad', as Ursula had called him, accustomed to high places, scornful of low, would be seen wielding an axe in a forest clearing and carting his own wood?

The rain had stopped. There was no sound in the clearing save the rhythmless fall of drops caught on twigs and branches, then finding their own way to last year's rotting leaves. Jolland was alone. Perhaps he had always been alone but now he knew it positively for the first time.

It was not his 'seeing' but his common sense that told him where his brother had been all these years; or why, coming again to what he remembered, he came secretly.

On that day of battle, that summer day, he had not drowned as had seemed the only possibility. He had most surely been taken by the Spanish. It had happened before – many English had been taken in raids by French or Dutch. Where had he been unless in Spain? And why had he returned now, unheralded, save as the servant and envoy of a new master? He would not be the first renegade Englishman to prosper in such service, nor the first to bring his mother tongue back to such a place as this where men were skilled in the manufacture of arms. Those who knew of these things, knew that Spain was bound to strike again, and their certainty had crept by devious ways about the countryside and into the towns. Few Englishmen expected other than a renewed onslaught, however little urgency the matter found in their daily lives.

It was in such times of waiting that an enemy deployed his spies.

In his anguish, Jolland pressed his face against the wet ground, not knowing where he should turn. Who should help him now? Now he needed a father's wisdom, and his own was far away, while Richard Medley, loved and respected, was gone for ever. Who should he turn to? Not, most certainly, to his cousin Ursula's husband, so strange and uncertain in his ways. And Master Piers was old. He was easily distressed, and though he was a vigorous, striding, sometimes stern old man, he was already past his seventieth year and was losing his authority. All the vagary and sadness of passing time crowded Jolland's mind then; he seemed to feel himself ageing. He thought how this morning Piers Medley had harked after his eldest brother, and how, not such long years ago, there had been those three brothers and their father thrusting and shouting about Mantlemass and Ghylls Hatch. He saw for the first time how both places were declining, the servants fewer, the farm growing smaller as the needs of the household decreased, the land less tended. Piers went less and less to Ghylls Hatch as he grew increasingly estranged from Robin – it had almost suprised Jolland to learn that he had ridden there this morning. Strives Minnis, that had become almost a part of Mantlemass, was already as good as lost; while another property, Tillow Holt, set among the waste edges of the forest, had so decayed and tumbled that it would never be reclaimed.

And now – what might not threaten Plashets?

Jolland had not greatly loved his brother Humfrey, who had bullied and belittled him, nor very greatly mourned his absence. All the anguish of that time had been in the terror of knowing not only that he had gone but knowing that he must return. The return had sounded out its threat, even then, far ahead of time, making the whole occasion sinister and uncomprehended. It was surely comprehended now.

Hard thinking came to his aid. He remembered who he was now and thrust the past away, letting the urgent present claim him. He thought how Master Richard had counselled him, at the very beginning of his tutorship to pause and think, and then to think deeply yet again before acting. To eschew impulse, though that might be thought slow. 'It cannot be enough,' he had once said, 'to measure with the eye alone.'

The eye with which Jolland measured now was his seeing eye. But then, seeming to hear Master Richard's voice speaking these words, it was as if the seeing eye closed, and this time for ever – as if what it had shown him had finally blinded it.

Timothy Morphew was waiting for Mus' Jolland when he at last reached Plashets.

'I'm greatly behind my time!'

'I did puzzle you weren't here b'now, sir.'

'My horse took lame. Then I went by Strives. Widow Godman was sick, two, three days together.'

Timothy frowned. His father, Dan Morphew, had been Lilias's furnaceman long years, ever since she came from her husband's working at Froreden, which was well into Kent. Timothy therefore remembered her all the days of his life, and would sometimes recall Ursula's childhood that ran alongside his own. When he was still not much more than a lad he had made Lilias a great fireback that still stood in the ingle at Strives. In his later years he had perfected this particular skill, designing moulds of both strength and delicacy. The needs of standing for some time as deputy to a young master, as he had sworn to Richard Medley he would do, had divorced him from his chosen work. He bore no malice, being very far from what was known hereabouts as 'a gridgen man'. He was part of industry, part of iron, part of the Medleys. That one blue eye that was so quick and keen showed concern when he spoke of Lilias Godman.

'How's she fare this day?' he asked. 'In better health, that I do trust.'

'Aye. So I bluv.' Jolland frowned. 'That Nance Tester seem a strange body.'

'She grow tip-tongued wi' living indoors,' Timothy replied scornfully – rather as if he spoke of a dog taken in to lie by the hearth. 'The Master should've took a better than Nance to care for her. As for that misagift son o' her'n – I'd not trust him a spit's length.'

Jolland shrugged slightly. He began to move away down the bank towards the furnace, Timothy following.

There was much work in progress at Plashets. There was a need to get ahead while the ponds were flush from winter snow and rain, for even a modest summer would diminish the flow. They had always turned out a great deal of domestic work at Plashets, it overtopped their manufacture of armament, even though at times that had been considerable. In the months after the Spanish were beaten off, restrictions had been set upon the production of guns, since their export must advantage an enemy. It had always been so, and to restrict export meant a restriction on home resources, too. The chief conflict was in fact with those who depended on wood for a living and saw the forests being cleared for making charcoal to fire the furnaces. For them a restricted export seemed a promise for the future. But one way, t'other way, as even Master Richard had agreed, the forest was a long day's travel from the lawgivers.

Today guns were uppermost in Jolland's mind. Cauldrons and firebacks, scythes and ploughs seemed unimportant.

'What state's our gun stock come to by this?' he asked Timothy. 'Still well stored and seen to?'

'In straw in the covered pit, sir,' Timothy answered, looking a shade surprised. His eye sparked. 'Off to war, are we, Mus' Jolland?'

'See the stuff looked over. See it secure. Do you understand? Most safe and secure. There's danger even when all's peace at home.'

'Surelye.' Since Jolland said no more and yet looked so nett-up with his own thoughts, Timothy remarked that the stuff was good stuff – a fine forging that he was proud to know bore the Plashet's trademark, even though it might not be shipped.

'There's two-three small cannon come here from Strives

– did you know that, master? In his last days, rest him, my father had a process different from any other – many'd've been glad of it, however masterly of themselves. Strives Master had it writ down – Dame Ursula did that. They never made only the two-three, and my father's dead, and Strives worked out. So only the widow know what she know and she's most like forgot.'

'Who's that?' Jolland said, sudden and sharp, as a man crossed the open land below and entered the furnace house.

'That's what I come to tell – when I met you, justly. That fellow come asking work this forenoon.'

'He was at Mantlemass sooner.'

'And asked work?'

'I sent him off. His hands were too clean.'

'I did think that. But old Thomsett took sick a day ago, so we're short a furnaceman.'

'He said he was a smith. Either way he's a foreigner. What'll our men say to that?'

'Naun. Time was they'd have him thrown out. But – naun.' Timothy looked awkwardly at Jolland. 'Come I made a boffle I'll send him on his way.'

'He can stay till Thomsett's hale again. But let'm know it.'

Timothy accepted the sharp tone with satisfaction. It pleased him greatly to know that Mus' Richard had made his pupil a man of purpose. He saw, too, that the young man was looking exceedingly weary. He'd send a lad to Ghylls Hatch for a horse to carry him home, he told Jolland.

'Thank you for your good thought, Timothy Morphew. But I told Dick Ade that I'd go on my own two hooves – and that mean here and back agin. Get to work, then. We've nabbled half the day.'

When Jolland and Timothy went through the working, the man Watkyn looked away and pretended to know nothing. He was with others at the furnace, in its second day of blowing. The smell of charcoal, of intense heat, the power of the bellows that seemed likely to send that heat so high that the furnace must burst asunder, kept every man tense and watchful. The furnace was a monster to be fed, and fed on what it craved, lest it spew all forth in disgust. From time to time the flame flared out like a great hank of destruction, and when that happened every man there, though he might be standing his own length away, grabbed at his leather cap and rammed it down to his ears. Sparks flew. The heat grabbed at the throat and nostrils. Now stripped to the waist and wrapped round in a great leather apron, Watkyn's muscle apparent, his hands that Jolland had doubted were now blackened. He moved with assurance, a barrel of a man, easy and confident.

As a general rule Jolland dearly loved to see the men working by the furnace. Today he was glad to leave and get out into the air. The rain had ceased, the sun was coming out, the birds were merry. It was a sad thing that his mood had to be so heavy. For an hour and more, he and Timothy Morphew sat together in the furnaceman's house, going over bills and accountings, and consulting about an order just brought in by the carrier, asking the cost of a pair of high courtyard gates.

By the time Jolland set out for home the sun was warm and the ground steamed gently after the rain. He moved down tracks wreathed in a delicate, capricious mist. Now he was anxious to be back at Mantlemass, and he took the shortest way. He had at least made some sort of decision. Whatever his brother might be about it could not be good or he would have declared himself. Master Piers must be told.

He was very weary indeed and limping wretchedly by the time he went indoors. As he came into the hall he was instantly aware that things were not as usual. There was some sort of bustle, and voices were raised on the floor above. The girl Ade, pretty Joan Ade, Dick's sister who had come to service in the house, ran down the stairs and cried out when she saw him.

'Mus' Jolland, sir – Dame Ursula look for you long ago! Pray hurry to her!'

'What's amiss? Is she sick? Or the children . . .?'

'Master Piers, sir. Rid up from Ghylls Hatch somewhere at noon – and took swimey – and were carried to his bed . . .'

The weariness left Jolland. He went up the stairs fast, striding, his mind racing with a terrible question: Am I to be alone after all? Must I be the one to act . . .?

'Be calm,' Ursula said. 'Better. He's better now.'

'What come to him?'

'He rid up from Ghylls Hatch. I see him much bothered – his voice strange and roupy. But he'd say nothing. He come up the stairs to his own chamber – and was suddenly crying out there was a great pain at his heart. He fell. He could not rise for a time.'

'As if he were dying . . .'

'All but. But do take cheer. I tell you he's near whole again. The pain went quickly. He's slept and he's woken and begun roaring to be let about his business. Only Agnes wunna let him.' She smiled. 'So you see he seem well enough now.'

She had come to meet him at the turn of the stairs. He leant against the banister, trying to steady himself against this, feeling all but ready to drop to the ground – the double burden seemed so heavy.

'You went afoot all day,' Ursula said.

'Pilgrim's lamer than I am.'

'One of the maids saw you go and was quite put-about.'

'What if he die? What shall come to you and me and Mantlemass then?'

'He is an old man, cousin,' she said gently. 'He must die soon. We know it and he knows it, too – how should it be otherly? You are Master Richard's heir and Plashets is yours now, save in final sealing. There shall be no heir for Master Piers, for my husband is no true son to him. Once it did seem so – and that was the Robin Medley I took so merrily for my husband. You cannot see it now – but so it was. Then all changed. Sometimes I bluv his mind is not his own ... But, God willing, you and I shall see Mantlemass safe. And when you take a wife, then she shall be my daughter as much as Susan. It shall be a new beginning. We shall make it so. We shall be strong between us. I swear it. Your father gave you to me. Your own mother could not love you dearer. And so I say we shall be strong together. We must be strong.'

The words poured from her, fermented by the intensity that had come with her fear for Master Piers. She was very pale.

'Give me your hand,' she said. 'Swear with me to save Mantlemass for my grandchildren.'

'On my honour before God,' he said, very low. 'I swear I shall do what I must.'

'Now,' she said, 'come speak with him and cheer him.'

Piers Medley was stretched on his bed, pillows at his back and a coverlet over his knees. His boots lay where they had been tossed when he was helped to bed. He looked so much more himself than Jolland had expected that the fear of the last moments seemed out of place and inopportune – as if they had set about burying a living corpse. Agnes Goodale sat at the bedside, with a porringer in one hand and spoon in the other. She was looking already less sorry than exasperated.

'What was it upset him?' Jolland asked under his breath, as he and Ursula came into the room.

'He'll not say. I'll leave you with him. Maybe he's ready to tell b'now.'

'It is for your *good*,' Agnes was saying. 'It is that very restoring posset that Widow Godman brews. It is to strengthen the blood.'

'Wine'll do that – and faster. I'm no puling babe, Agnes Goodale, to be fed wi' a spoon. Fetch me some wine!'

Agnes rose, pulling down the corners of her mouth, frowning and shrugging.

'How d'you fare now, sir?' Jolland asked. He went near and bent to touch the old man's hand, calling him so in his mind for the first time. The hand was shaking slightly against the cover. 'I'm sorry to see you low, Master Piers.'

'There's naun food and wine'll not do for my body. My mind's clear, I thank Christ – though it do dread what it know.'

'What does it know that troubles you?'

Piers gave a sharp laugh and the good colour rushed up into his face in the most miraculous fashion.

'Dear lad,' he said, 'you sound as prim and picksome as the Staglye parson!'

Jolland flushed, glancing at Ursula, who seemed to have smothered a laugh.

'We'll fetch some wine, Agnes,' she said, beckoning the other woman from the room, nodding in a meaningful fashion at Jolland as she went.

'I'm no holy man,' Jolland said as the door closed, 'but I'll still ask what troubles you so sore?'

Piers groaned. He pushed back the covers and swung

his legs over the side of the bed – then stayed clinging to the bedpost so hard that the tester swayed and the curtains shook.

'My life's bin full of boffles, cousin. There was only once, ever, in all the years, I did what I should. I'm not confessing my sins ... It's the mistakes come hard to think of. The judgement that was weak. The trust placed different than was wise. I see it – and see no end to it.' He paused, shaking his head as if somehow to clear his vision. 'Robin,' he said. 'Robin called Medley.' His voice sank so low Jolland had to strain to hear it. 'Today I cursed him as once I cursed Robin Halacre, his father.'

The bitterness of Piers's tone made Jolland shiver and sicken. What more was to come of today?

'You were at Ghylls Hatch, sir ...?'

'I had a need to ride out. Hearing of my brother Harry – Well, who know if the fellow spoke true? Maybe Harry lives still, but lets his son be master ...' He paused a moment, thinking about this, then shook his head, saying it sounded very little like the Harry Medley he remembered.

Again he paused, his head in his hands, as if it were so heavy it needed just now to be carried. He went on after what seemed minutes, his voice torn and wretched.

'I sent Ghylls Hatch to ruin that day I let Robin be master there. Years and years I saw he'd never do well enough. There was his father coming out in him. He was like two men fighting between themselves. Disappointment's a hard thing to bear, cousin. I banished it and let him be. Isn't it said that trust given is promise fulfilled?'

'Aye, sir.' He waited, but again Piers stayed silent. 'What come to Ghylls Hatch, then, sir?'

'As I – as I rode out I met old Bunce coming here. Red

in the face. Half dead wi' rage. He's older than I am ... This first light, he tell me – this very morning, Jolland, every horse in the place bin rounded up save Iris and Pilgrim – even my old Drummer, poor beast that was so good and true ...' Now his voice rose and strengthened as anger took him. 'Rid off in a train this first light, all the lot, Robin at the head, but half a dozen men come from London – so they tell. And why in God's name could you not speak sooner? I bawled out. Because, for sure, Master Robin said I knew of it – and since I did ever bid to make him master there, and time and often refuse to make his answers for'm – who's to blame but only Piers Medley – fool and simpleton! Fool! Fool! Fool! Blockhead!'

'We'll get after them!' Jolland cried wildly.

'Wi' Iris? And lame Pilgrim? I'm not the only fool, seems me. They'd been hours gone already when I came to know of it!'

'Where'd they be going?'

'London men in it? Who'd say? There's been talk over years of fighting in Ireland – expeditions planned by great men ... My lord Essex ... It's been spoke often enough in the town and the markets, over and over. Our beauties could be shipped, then.'

The fullness of the disaster seemed to strike him anew. He cried out bitterly again and again, covering his face and weeping, if not with tears yet inwardly.

'My whole life is gone. My life is gone before God end it.' He groped for Jolland's hand and grasped it. 'Fetch my daughter. I must speak with her soon. Now. Tell Ursula fetch her mother here ...'

This sounded so confused that Jolland sprang to the door and flung it open, shouting to Ursula to come quickly, then running back to Master Piers.

'Twice before this,' Piers was muttering. 'Twice

destroyed. But this time – this time for ever.'

Jolland knew no way of comforting him. Indeed he could only add to the terrible mounding up of trouble if he told his own tale. He looked with anguish at the old man, remembering how only that morning he had thought of the decline besetting the fortunes of Medley of Mantlemass. He had counted then what was lost already. Now he must add Ghylls Hatch to the bitter sum.

9

Piers

'Agnes shall go,' Ursula said. 'Better I stay near.' She told Agnes to be urgent, but if possible not to alarm Lilias. 'She's been less than herself, so my cousin say. It's hard to move her, once she come stubborn. But come you think best, Agnes, then let her be frit.'

'I'm the one like to be frit,' said Agnes. 'It's dark night, b'now.'

'It's near moonrise – but get lanterns and take one of the men with you. She must be fetched here, one way t'other way. Master Piers need her sore now. She ever did delight him.'

Strangely so, too, Ursula thought, as Agnes went off on her errand. In the old days it had been Lilias's sharp sardonic humour that had made him laugh and cheered him out of any dump he was in. But lately she had so turned in upon herself, and so obstinately refused to live at Mantlemass, that she was the one who had seemed to be needing comfort.

'Let you and me stay calm,' Ursula said to Jolland, when they were alone. 'The world's gone mad – let you and me stay sane, for God's sweet sake.'

'I never thought to see him look so beaten ...'

'Robin Medley did this to him. If he die – then Robin Medley killed him. This is my husband, surelye – but I came long past to care nothing for him. That should be thought wicked – for wives are to stay true though husbands grow false as hell. The wickedness is all in him. And I pray to God with all my heart and soul that I never set eyes on Robin Medley from this day on.'

He said nothing, only nodded. Too much had happened for him to be more appalled than he was already.

'Go up to him, Jolland. Stay till my mother come. Only – call me if need be ... Let me alone a little.'

She watched him go, frowning after him, knowing that not the least of her fears lay with him – or grew from him. His sudden talk of his brother, his insistence on having seen him ... If by some chance or miracle Humfrey Jolland still lived, would he not be knocking on the door, seeking his brother? And how should he come to the forest without first going to his father's house in London? Indeed, why should he come in this fashion to the forest? He could not know that his brother lived now at Mantlemass unless he had been already to his father – and if so, why should he skulk without discovering himself? Like Jolland, she saw only one answer – that he had escaped drowning to be taken prisoner by the Spanish, that he had lived ever since in that country, learning other ways, taking service with a foreign master. Men had so changed allegiance, as well she knew. And returning as spies, seeking to subvert workers hereabouts who knew only one loyalty, had lost their lives darkly and secretly, murdered by those who experienced no grievance, who never questioned the allegiance to which they had been born. But however staunch the majority, there were always the one or two who might be tempted for some personal reason – a grudge, perhaps such as could have been engendered by Jolland only yesterday, when he raged over a botched job. What might that man answer if tempted to betrayal of some secret process, or the removal by night of arms to be shipped fast down river to the open sea? Or there had been that time when Master Richard turned off red-headed Henty, and later worried that he had done ill in the matter ... And if there seemed little reason for Humfrey Jolland to betray his own kinsmen, it was not to be denied that men were swayed in many ways, some beyond their power to defeat. By gratitude, by fear – by exchange of service, such as buying freedom in return for performing some mission ...

As she considered this, walking restless and impatient about the hall, much more came to toss and batter Ursula's already bruised and tender thoughts. She recalled the man Watkyn, who seemed to know much and yet somehow too little. She thought of her husband, remembering with revulsion his accusation of Master Piers. She had never allowed herself to think of it again till now, it had so angered her. Yet Robin must have kept it ever before him, until it had made him so mad he had coldly set about the final ruin of Ghylls Hatch, that had been the better part of Piers Medley's life. Even until today, Ursula had kept some small doubt about Robin's being in fact Piers's own son, at first unacknowledged and then by some trick of circumstance regained. She could never think so again, and now she was glad of what she would have once regretted.

She sat down and tried to think calmly, to force her memory, which was struggling over some half-lost recollection.

Because she had recalled red-headed Henty, so now she recalled the name in another connection – for it was old

Goody Henty who had spoken to Robin of his father's death and the manner of it. She had done this long after the event; after her kinsman had been sent packing?

The face of treachery took sudden shape, and set itself upon the shoulders of four men – Robin Medley and Henty, Watkyn; and Humfrey Jolland, who wore it like a mask over features she could not recall.

She sat very still, her hands tightly clasped together. She had done as she had intended, mustered her thoughts, remembered what she needed, set all in order. It was still possible that only her fears and fancies had combined to show her this picture, but she was calm enough now to think not. She stayed a long time, her mind and her muscles all clenched over these deliberations, so that she almost felt that the world sat on her shoulders and she might never move again. She rose with difficulty and began again pacing and turning, trying, this time, to see what needed to be done. Where were the horses? Had they indeed been taken to London, or were they to be shipped from some port along the south coast? For Spain? Or might they rather be maintained in hiding further west, ready to assist some planned invasion? A small exploratory expedition, perhaps, such as had taken place before this in the west country.

And where about the forest were those four traitors of hers gathered and waiting? Who gave them lodging? How should they be taken and cheated of their purposes? What of Jolland himself? Must he be required to betray in his turn, to condemn his own brother? As she was thinking now, quite coldly, of condemning her own husband. He still was her husband, and her children's father . . .

She found herself, her eyes tight closed, praying for guidance – then checked miserably as she realized what her petition meant . . .

After an hour or so, Jolland came down to her.

'He sleeps and wakes. Each time he wakes, he asks for your mother.'

'She'll not be here for another hour at best.'

'Cousin – he is very sick.'

'I know it. It come so sudden.'

'Jane Bunce is there. And old Goody Awcock.'

'See who stays in the kitchen. You'd best eat.'

As they spoke thus quietly together, the situation seemed to change its colour. It grew from a state of nervous alarm, as when Piers had first been taken ill, to one of calm and tragic anticipation. Their low voices and solemn eyes accepted now what they had at first impatiently rejected – indeed had barely contemplated. He is an old man, Ursula had said. He must die soon ... But he was dying already. He was dying now. Soon was now.

'He never took sick ever before that I know of, Jolland. His heart is quite broken. Robin broke it for him.' Under her breath she said, 'My husband Robin that was once ... My once-love Robin ...'

Jolland stood by her and spoke close to her ear.

'Shall we be strong enough?'

'Aye. We shall. Not only for this.'

'What else?' he asked, very still.

'I see now why you spoke of your brother. I see the stranger may be your brother. Maybe I took up that seeing eye of yours. The Spanish took him from the sea – and now they send him to pay for his life wi' guns ... Is that how you would answer?'

He nodded. He was ageing as they stood there, his young manhood that had but lately grown from his boyhood turning now to maturity.

'They might kill him,' Ursula said. 'You know that.

Morphew – Penfold – the other Awcock. Young Hendall. No Medleys ever were betrayed. Not the master of Strives, neither. Till now. Till now ... What's that? Is my mother here already?'

There were voices outside, but before Ursula could run to the door, Agnes came in. She moved very swiftly, but without flurry; Agnes never did flurry or wring her hands.

'What happened, Agnes? There and back so soon ... Is my mother wi' you?'

'I took a loan of her old pony to get home.'

'Then she's not come?'

'Your mother bides at home.'

'She would not come? When you told her he asks for her? He is very ill ... But of course it is late. She was abed. She'll come in the morning, no doubt? We must all pray she come in time.'

'You must fetch her to Mantlemass, lady,' Agnes said earnestly. 'She was not gone to bed – but she'd as well've been. Nance said she took over much of her bedtime posset – a heady draught, Nance say, and great care needed. I see clear that your mother should not be there, all but alone at Strives – and mixing and brewing and tasting her herbs and roots and spices. There's danger in it. She sat there stupefied and neither could hear nor speak! It was pitiful. I never saw the like or anything near, and pray I need never again.'

'Oh Agnes, what's come to us all this day? I rose up easy, like on any other morning. The sun shone ... The children watched the ducks ... Where's that world now?'

'Lilias?' Piers asked, quite strongly, as Ursula came into the room.

She was immediately cheered, and bent over him smiling.

'It is Ursula, sir. It is very late. In the morning. She'll be here in the morning.'

He was silent a moment, looking into her face and frowning. Then peering round the room and seeing the other two women still there, he said quietly, 'God shall bless that pair – but send them packing. Since your mother's not come I have to speak with you instead.'

The two women went at once, the young matron looking tearful, the old woman shaking her head and pursing her lips.

'You never saw me take to my bed till this,' Piers said, irritable rather than dismayed.

'You'll soon be well . . .'

'No.'

'Yes. Yes – you have to be patient.'

'An end's easier seen than a beginning.'

She frowned uncertainly, knowing his meaning, finding it strangely put.

'What beginning?' she asked, unwilling to speak of an end.

He pulled himself up in the bed, pausing halfway, grunting and putting his hand against his heart as if it might burst out and must be contained.

'In the little chamber,' he said, struggling. 'My own room. Bring the small chest to me here. You know the one.'

'The little iron-bound chest . . .?'

'Bring it.'

The room which had been the centre of Piers's existence, where he worked on Ghylls Hatch matters and the concerns of Mantlemass, was up a twist of stair. In the early days of Mantlemass, before they put a floor across the hall to make more rooms, it had been part of the solar. At the time of the alterations the little window, through which the ladies of the household could look down upon the comings and goings in the hall below, had been filled in. Perhaps it had never been used for its true purpose, for styles in building had changed fast at the time Mantlemass was built, since ways and manners of living had changed, too. Piers had slept in the room as a young boy, then later when it was enlarged had shared it with his young brother Richard. Before that, his father had had it for his own when he first came to Mantlemass under the wing of Master Lewis Mallory.

In this small room, Piers and Richard and their cousin, Susannah Mallory, had worked over the old books that almost burnt when Ghylls Hatch was fired because of disease among the horses. They had laboured to trace old lines, that the once famous stables and stud might be built up once more. It was to be an inheritance for Robin – that eager and loving boy who had now, as a man, ruthlessly betrayed all that he should have been heir to . . .

Ursula took up the iron-bound box, finding it very little heavier than her own spirit.

Goody Awcock was outside Piers's door, standing uneasily with Jane Bunce, and with Joan Ade who had now joined them.

'He need a priest, madam,' the old woman said, almost in a whisper. 'For his soul's dear sake, lady – send to Staglye for the priest.'

'God bless you, goody,' Ursula replied. 'Pray ask Agnes to make up a draught for him – she'll know which . . . I'll speak with him as you wish . . . No! Leave it!' she said sharply to Joan, who had tried to take the box from her.

She went into the room and closed the door behind her, carrying the box to the small table pulled up to the bedside. Let him have it, he said; so she set it across his knees. Then she fetched candles and set them on the table.

'Sir,' she said tentatively, 'Goody Awcock is troubled for you.'

'She fret for my soul,' he said, near chuckling, but then catching his breath. 'Tell her – tell her I spoke wi' my Maker some hours back. I know him and he know me ... So let it rest.'

'As you wish it.'

'Now,' said Piers. He plucked at a thread he wore round his neck. 'Help me ...'

It was a tarnished gold thread, knotted here and there where it had worn thin, and on it there dangled a small, almost pretty key.

'I lost the first,' he said. 'Dan Morphew wrought this. My daughter's furnaceman. A delicate hand when he list.'

'My mother's furnaceman,' Ursula said, unwilling to correct him, but even less willing to think he was rambling. 'Dan Morphew, you said. Father to Timothy – Plashet's Morphew.'

'Very stiff ... Unlock it for me.'

She turned the key and opened the lid on a jumble of papers that could not immediately mean anything to her. But as he picked up this one and that, shuffling them very slowly with shaking hands, she saw many finely written lists, and recognized the names of Ghylls Hatch horses. And there was a drawing made in charcoal of what was now called 'the Plashet's Lily', that had once been her mother's trademark at Strives Minnis.

Piers stopped turning the papers. His hands rested on the contents of the box and there was a slight rustling sound as they moved together under his fingers that could not be quite still, an old man's hard, chilling skin rasping faintly on the parchment. Ursula waited, thinking sadly that maybe he could no longer concentrate and had forgotten what he had been going to say. The room, dark beyond the bed since she had moved the candles, was so empty that it frightened her.

'Shall I call Jolland?'

'No.'

'You said you would tell me some thing or other,' she suggested, hoping to help him. 'Is it the horses? I see some names writ there.'

'More than that . . . Wait a little. I forget . . .'

But then immediately he rallied in a manner almost miraculous. 'Firstly, my mind's clear as frore water. Your mother is my daughter. She is my true daughter. None know this but she.' He put his hand, shaking as it was, quite firmly on hers, and said in a gentle voice, almost shy, 'That make you my granddaughter. Should that greatly trouble you?'

At this strange moment Agnes came to the door with the drink Ursula had sent for.

'Let me bring it to him,' she said, as Ursula opened the door, her face so bewildered and lost that for a moment Agnes feared that Master Piers was dead.

'Give it to me, Agnes. Shut the door now and go away. Pray understand. It must be so.'

She returned to the bed, saying as if she had neither understood nor heard his last words,

'Drink this. It will help the pain.'

Only her voice, always very loving when she spoke to him, held now so much of warmth, of a deep delight, that he could not doubt she had understood.

At the end of a long strange hour, slow and difficult and full of mystery, Ursula rose from Piers Medley's bedside. She called in the women who had been all this time waiting outside.

'He'll sleep, so he say. Stay with him. Call me when he

wake – pray, call me at once.'

She took up the little chest and carried it back to the room over the hall. The key on its gold thread hung now about her own neck, secret as he had wished it to be. She set the chest back in its place, but lingered with her hands on the lid, as if reluctant to leave it. It held so much of wonder that she knew she must stay quiet for a little and think of the things Piers had told her, the injunctions he had laid upon her. First, that she should never in her life speak of the deepest secret to any but her own chosen kin, son or daughter as she saw fit, but then only when she felt her own death near. Second, to take the shabby leatherbound book of Latin poems that was in the box, and by some means contrive that it come into the hands of his brother Harry's family, whichever of his sons now held authority; for far to the west, in that other forest where men prised iron from the stone, would be found the only true Medley blood, and therefore the heir to Mantlemass.

'I swear it shall be done,' she had said. 'Howsoever, one way, t'other way, it shall be done.'

'Lawyers,' he said, 'Sir Francis will know – he will know how best . . . Tell why you must know, but never speak of – of the other. Just say – my wish . . . The heir, tell him . . .'

Then, after a long pause, he had said that if his brother's family came to Mantlemass, she must not fear. She should trust her kin to accept the obligation laid upon them. Mantlemass was her home, and her children's home, not only till any other claim it, but after.

If she felt faint doubt at this, wondering if he saw his kin and hers at this time too kindly, she did not let it trouble her. There were others who would see her safe.

Then he had told her, when he died, to take the great ring from his finger at once. It was the ring they called *the lark and the laurel.*

'It come from my mother's father – and first from his ... God forgive me, I took it from him ... It was for a token ... for a love token.' He was silent, as if remembering. Then he said – 'Cherish it. Cherish this ring ... Always ... Keep it for Mantlemass ...'

Ursula rose now from her knees by the box. She went from the room and locked the door behind her, slipping that key into her pocket for safety. She wished she might speak to no one, but knew that Jolland would be waiting anxiously after all this time.

It was now very late. The house glimmered with the light of the few lanterns hung against the walls, which ordinarily would by this hour be dark. The dusky light added to the strangeness and mystery of the occasion – the mystery of death and that other mystery of which he had told her. Ursula went slowly downstairs feeling half disembodied, her kinship fresh upon her, her knowledge of far stranger matters spinning through her mind.

Jolland heard her coming and rose at once from the settle where he had been huddled, shivering, for he had let the fire die.

'Well?'

'He's sleeping.'

'He's better!'

'No.'

'Is there no physician can help him?'

'Here? In this deep place?'

'The town – I'll ride to the town. Or to London ...'

'Where's that eye now that you saw so clear with?' she asked, faintly smiling. 'You of us all must see the way he go.'

'That eye's bin blinded, cousin.'

'Let be,' she said, sighing. 'I see death coming other times. It look justly so and no other way. God wills it and so it is.'

'Shall I go to him now?'

'Wait a little. They'll call when he wakes.'

She moved away and he was about to follow her but she shook her head. She went back up the stairs, but this time to her own bedchamber. It was here, at a little desk that one of the men about the place had made her, that nowadays she sat to write in her book. And so now she set out lights, and sat down there, and cut a new pen and began to write. For what if some disaster struck her down, as it had struck Master Piers – then the secret could be lost forever, for her mother who knew it could not be certainly trusted to keep a clear mind.

'When Master Piers Medley was on his death bed,' she wrote carefully, 'he sent for me and kept me close with him while he told this tale: That my mother Lilias Godman was his natural daughter; and so I was his grandchild. I was not, as I had once been let suppose, his daughter by marriage, since my husband, Robin, was Medley only by adoption; he had lived since childhood as Master Piers's son, but was in fact the son of a boyhood friend of Master Piers, named Halacre. So then, Master Piers said to me, the true line of inheritance go through my brother Harry, who took his own way, many years past.'

Here Ursula paused. She wondered how much she should write down. She wrote a line or two more, then came to the next matter, how he had said she must never doubt she shared his blood,

'In that blood, says he, lieth the strange secret that come to us from my father's father, and from his father . . . This secret he told my mother, and now told me, and the matter of it was held in an old book, where a certain name was written . . .'

Here again she paused, for the tale of the book and of

Harry Medley's family could not yet be told. So she left a clear half page that might be added to, and continued on a new, clean page, partly for her own sake, to see it set out clear and unmistakeable.

'In the book is writ the true secret. It is the name *Plantagenet.* This is the blood that come to me through my mother, secret daughter to Master Piers Medley. It come to him from his father, who founded his line, who had it from his father in turn. That man told he was natural son to England's king, and had spoke with him once on the eve of a great battle . . .'

Ursula read this again and again. But she saw it had best not be written here. She would write it, rather, in some fashion in the book itself. A secret needed to be contained only in one place – and so should this one be. She cut out the page neatly and carefully and burnt it at the candle on the desk. After this she sat a long time with her head bowed on her hands, at once bitterly sorrowful yet full of gladness, not for any high blood, but simply that she shared it with Piers. And she thought of other things he had told her: How his wife, Isabella, had died tragically, leaving him with one daughter, Catherine, whom Ursula had known when she still lived at Mantlemass. So, when he was young, just widowed, he met her grandmother, for whom Lilias had named her Ursula. Of this he spoke little, saying only, painfully, that she would not wed him, and years went by before he learned that she had borne his daughter.

With perhaps even greater pain he told of that first Robin, Robin Halacre, his boyhood friend, his family humble weavers. That Robin had grown ambitious, clawing his way among great men until he was himself the judge and arbiter between living and dying. Time had overtaken him, and though he fled at a change of royal power and religious practice, an enemy from his days of power found him out and contrived him a traitor's death at Tyburn ... Here again the story broke off. Piers had said only that he had hated Robin Halacre, who had harmed too many; but Piers had never wronged him, as he knew some old body had accused him. The hatred had troubled his conscience, so that when Halacre died, his children had been brought to Mantlemass.

'I did come to love this boy for my own,' Piers said, just before he slept, exhausted. 'Loving is a great and sore undoer of strong purpose.'

Ursula did not write this, and never would do so, for she could not know all the truth. Nor was the tale of Robin Halacre and his son one she cared to leave for whoever came after. Better they should read those earlier pages, where she had written 'my love Robin', and fancifully set down the names of her children, some of whom had never been born, nor the others lived as long as she liked to remember them.

She thought of the three, sleeping now quietly in the night time – Lewis, Susan, Thomas. Which should hear what she had been told that day? Not Lewis ... It came into her mind, then, most strangely, perhaps because the terrors of the day had so battered and exhausted her, and now the small hours of another day had come, that what she had written was meant for some further future, some child of her own children. Maybe that unborn creature might feel for her the same warm flow of love across the generations as now she, Ursula Medley, felt for the grandfather she had only just discovered.

The idea pleased and comforted her. One day she would make her will, like any great and grand lady. This writing desk, in which she would always keep her book and all such papers and letters as seemed to connect her with her day and with Mantlemass, should be bequeathed to her first grandchild. Then she corrected herself: Her first granddaughter, rather, for women were born with little of their own, and the smallest inheritance gave dignity. Then all that was written down should bind this present to that future, finding her, too, a little earthly immortality.

She wrote, almost shyly, – *For my granddaughter.* It looked at once pleasing and a little absurd. And thinking how this unknown girl, who would have grown from her, would come to read what was written, she went over today's story carefully, correcting as best she knew, the spelling that often looked awkward.

In the writing desk, the pride of its maker, there was a little secret drawer. Ursula felt for the catch, so well concealed she never found it with ease, and at last it slid open. She took the key on its gold thread from around her neck. She cut a tag of paper and wrote on it: *Smalle chest.* Then she slipped the key into the drawer, and put away her book and her pen.

She heard someone coming to the door and knew it would be Agnes. She ran across the room and opened the door.

'He woke,' Agnes said. 'A moment since.'

'How do you find him?'

'Quiet. Calm. But come to him now. Best not delay.'

For a second Ursula paused. She leant towards Agnes, gripping her hands hard, resting against her and feeling her strength.

'Call my cousin, Agnes.'

She straightened herself, and crossed the floor to the far door that was the door of Master Piers Medley's bedchamber.

10

Master Medley's Favourite Son

When morning came, Ursula left Agnes and the rest to do what was needed and went to Strives in search of her mother. As she went, riding slowly on the old pony that Agnes had brought last night to Mantlemass, she saw that the tidings, in the way of such matters, were already about the forest. The men were coming up from Plashets, and their wives and children with them. They stood as she passed, the men with their caps in their hands, the women with downcast eyes, the children curious – they did not salute her, or speak, but stood with their heads bowed. When she had gone by they continued on their way, tramping to Mantlemass in silence still, to pay a last tribute to the Master.

Ursula had been too deeply saddened to weep. Now as she passed these other mourners, the tears filled her eyes and ran over. She rode on down the track crying bitterly, as one of her children might have done.

When she came in sight of Strives, she grew calm again. What lay ahead she could only dread, and she knew she needed all her patience and good sense.

Lilias came from the house when she saw her daughter,

but frowned at the sight of the pony.

'That's Folly you're riding. He never got loose and run to Mantlemass?'

Ursula dismounted and tethered the animal.

'Let me indoors,' she said. 'I have somewhat to tell. I have old Folly because Agnes rid him back last night. She come all the way through the dark to fetch you to Mantlemass.'

Lilias flushed. 'Through the dark? Then I were sleeping, surelye.'

'Mother – you must leave tasting and drinking your draughts and your potions.'

'I cannot sleep otherly,' Lilias said, shrugging but looking away.

'They fuddle like wine. And can kill quicker.'

'Let be!' Lilias was silent a moment, then frowned and seemed to become aware of what Ursula had first said. 'Why should Agnes Goodale come through the dark?'

'Master Piers asked for you.'

'So late . . . ?'

'He needed you sore, mother, and you could not come.'

'Well, well . . . Two-three hours . . . I'll come now.'

Ursula was wearing the big ring, *the lark and the laurel*, which she had taken off Piers Medley's hand as he had wished she should. It was thrust over her thumb, and now she pulled it off and held it out on her open palm towards her mother. She did not speak, for seeing it thus divorced from its owner, her grief struck her again and she had to struggle to stay calm.

Lilias stared at the ring. She put out her hand and took it, closing her fist on it and holding it against her heart, bowing her head, for the message was clear.

'He told me the secret, mother – that you are his daughter. And – and that other secret. He would not, had you bin there. But he needed to speak of it once again, so he tell, and make it secure. And safe enough in my keeping, you know that.'

Lilias huddled over the ring and could not speak, but rocked herself in a helpless, hopeless fashion.

'I know he give it long ago to your mother,' Ursula said, 'and how you bring it back to him that time you thought your daughter was like to wed wi' his son ... Did he tell you how he stole it off his own father, since he'd no other token for my grandmother Ursula?'

Lilias vaguely shook her head.

'I could 'a spoke wi' him again. Oh what come to him?'

'What you did ever say about my husband was truly thought,' Ursula said steadily, though it cost her much even now. 'That Robin I loved turned mad. He broke Piers Medley's heart. It is true, before God. My husband as good as struck him down, for he died of grief. I pray I need never see that sorry face again – but ask me no more of the doing, for I've no words to tell it.'

Lilias stretched out her hand and put it on Ursula's, but without speaking. They sat thus in silence together for a long while. None came to disturb them. About the house the forest was silent except for the birds. Sometimes when the wind was right, work in progress at Plashets was easily heard here at Strives. Today there was nothing, though any wind there was did come from that direction. The furnaces should have been blowing another three days after this one, but had been allowed to go dark as a mark of respect.

At last Ursula said, 'Come home with me now to Mantlemass. Wear the ring till you die. "Keep it for Mantlemass," he said.'

'I'll come – but not today. I'll not look on that dead face. I loved it living. I'll not pity it dead.'

'But promise. Give me your word.'

'I'll come to Mantlemass, daughter. I do swear it. In my own good time. But soon.'

'Well – God keep you, then. Do indeed let it be soon.'

Ursula left the house then. She still saw no sign of Nance or her son, so she let the pony out to graze and then turned for home. She would be glad to walk, for there was yet more to think of than the death of Piers Medley. In the disturbance the event must cause, evil intention could well find freedom to come and go.

At the turn of the track, Jolland was waiting for his cousin.

'Come with me. I'll show you that place I saw my brother.'

She turned at his side. They were both wearing dark cloaks and the overgrown track quickly received them.

'It's much trampled, I see, Jolland, for all the tangle. I never yet went this way that I recall. What shall you show me?'

'A dwelling.'

'A dwelling here on the forest – that I never saw?'

'Wait,' he said. 'Move softly.'

They went quietly, no wind here, the birds muted at the approach of noon. Their light and careful tread made little more noise than might a run of coneys. They came to the green bog and the climb over the rocky mound, where Jolland had thought there might be a cave. Then they were in sight of the clearing and he drew her deeper among the undergrowth. There they must pick their way, their cloaks catching on thorns.

He put out his hand suddenly, checking her, pulling her down to crouch behind a cluster of bushes, broom just budding. They made perfect cover, dense enough for concealment, yet giving a thousand slits through which the watchers might peer. And between the green fingers, the buds decking them as with rings, Ursula saw ahead of her a stone cottage – like most others about the forest, though with an air of being recently set in order. The chimney smoked comfortably. A few hens picked among the blackened remains of last year's nettles. Three ducks preened themselves by the small pond. The place looked like any other holding, poor and undistinguished; save for its fresh-laid thatch.

'*Here* you saw him?' Ursula whispered.

He nodded, but instantly caught her arm to silence her.

A man was coming down the further track. He carried two rabbits dangling in one hand, and a cudgel in the other. He was altogether familiar. He was Nance Tester's dunch son, Peter. He came up to the cottage, pausing very slightly to kick one of the hens out of his path, so that it went zig-zagging ahead of him squawking wildly; then he came to the door, and with no knock, lifted the latch and entered with an air of ease and familiarity.

'Nance?' Ursula said, almost to herself. 'How should Nance be in it?'

Her world, already rocking, seemed to swing like a bell's great clapper. She looked at Jolland in bewilderment and near despair. She knew what this place must be – Halacres; Robin's home in childhood.

Then they heard voices. The door opened. Peter came out as if shoved sharply from behind – and a following shout of laughter fitted the picture well. Peter was still carrying the rabbits. He took out a knife and bent to sharpen it on the step. Muttering and mumbling resentfully, he set about skinning the carcases, throwing the offal to the hens, but pocketing the skins. He looked over his shoulder nervously as he did so, and only seconds later the door opened and a young man came out. He said something they could not hear, then laughed. Peter laughed with him, but uneasily.

At first Ursula could not see the young man's face. She knew by Jolland's quickly caught breath who he must be. And when he turned, looking around him from side to side, as if he had heard some movement, she knew beyond doubt that she was looking at Humfrey Jolland. She was surprised to see the face of a traitor so pleasant and smiling. He was very like his father, his beard of similar trim, but his expression when the smile died was both worldly and rough. He no longer looked a gentleman's son.

Humfrey was hurrying Peter on with his job. Then a second man joined him at the door and they stood watching and taunting as Peter fumbled, then cut himself, then fumbled on. The second man was Watkyn.

All Ursula wanted now was to get away, to go home and find no worse than the sadness of Piers Medley's death. But they dared not move and risk discovery, for that would be no solution. It seemed a long time before Peter had finally jointed the rabbit and handed it over. Humfrey and Watkyn turned at once to go indoors – but Peter caught at Watkyn's sleeve, holding out his hand for payment.

Watkyn struck the hand aside and went into the cottage. Humfrey very slightly paused, and Ursula felt Jolland stiffen. Then Humfrey, too, shrugged and went indoors. Peter turned away for home, and after a bit they heard him crying, and watched him lumbering off, smearing with dirty blood-stained hands at his eyes and nose.

This time it was Ursula who checked Jolland.

'Let him go. Come we need him, he's ours for the asking.'

For the next days there was quiet on the forest. The coffin lay that time in the chapel barn, called so because it had been begun as a chapel then abandoned when the times made it inexpedient. For three days and nights, men and women came and went, most of them known, and their families for years before, but also many strangers – even from the town. The parson from Staglye came stumping up the hill, and rated Ursula that she had not sent for him, and raged, too, at other matters – being one of the new men with new ways. Many small tributes had been laid upon the coffin and around it – like primrose garlands, branches new-leafed, swags of bluebells, the golden broom that had burst into flower during the warm days just past, that held for Ursula and Lilias a double meaning. But there were other offerings, strange as ancient magic that was said to be forgotten now. Like the robin's nest with its clutch of eggs, a pitiful sacrifice; like the peregrine falcon, its wings pinned outspread, an arrow still in its breast. And there was a squirrel, set up as if it lived; the antlers of a hart-royal; many horseshoes. Also a great iron lantern, burning when it was left and ever replenished.

None knew which mourner brought which offering, but all were bitterly condemned by the new man from Staglye.

'Is this a heathen god you worship? And am I to bury him in consecrated ground?'

'Let it be at the crossroads then!' cried Ursula. 'God will judge you as well as he judge Piers Medley and all that seek to honour him.'

'Grief makes you bold, dame! Well – I will let him in. But send your own men to dig the grave, for none of mine shall.'

Timothy Morphew, Simon Hendall, Old Awcock, Youngest Ade went to dig Piers's grave. They dug it where the graveyard sloped a little from its ancient mound. The forest was out of sight there, but the land lay open to the weather and there were others of his family at hand . . .

'I do pray my father be in time,' Jolland said.

They had sent word by the courier who, riding through from the town, made the journey to London once in every week, with a satchel of letters and messages slung over his shoulder. The day was never certain, and Dick Ade had waited for him many hours, not knowing if he waited in vain.

At midday, three days after Piers Medley died, Sir Francis Jolland rode in to Mantlemass. The lid of the coffin was then lifted for the last time, and that night was the burial.

There was a moon but a shutter of fine cloud obscured it. The cloud diffused the light and all the sky was starless yet faintly glowing. The spring day had been warm but was chill by dusk, so that delicate wisps of mist rose along the banks of the streams and lay over ponds and under trees – yet freakishly stirring and drawing back, then swirling to a man's height but no higher.

The order into which the mourners fell came about without any plan or instruction. At the head of the procession, Ursula rode Iris at a walking pace, Jolland on foot beside her. Lilias, too, was mounted, and Francis Jolland walked with her, his hand on old Folly's bridle. The coffin rode on a waggon, but the tracks being still soft from winter, it was necessary more than once for the cortège to pause. The coffin was then lifted and carried, and the waggon shoved and tugged on its way till the coffin could be taken up again.

Behind the coffin followed a crowd of forty or fifty, all on foot, workers and servants of the house, and neighbours from further west whose animals had grazing on the forest, in some cases Mantlemass tenantry. Most carried torches and sometimes the light mist wreathed them, then fell and

dispersed, cut down by the flames. Some women bore lanterns that bobbed modestly a little below the noble flare of the torches. They went, perhaps strangely, not altogether in silence, but speaking quietly among themselves, saying most often, *I remember him one day ... He come by my door and stop to speak ... He did this, he did that ... When Ghylls Hatch burn down that time – they say his heart near broke that time ...* But none spoke of the reason why this time he could not recover. That name was never mentioned; and though for all the years there had been plenty to smile and say it was a wise child that knew his own father, yet now they would not have allowed that interloper to claim the least jot of Medley blood. Word had got about soon enough, with the Ghylls Hatch men raging around the forest of the horses stolen away. Whether or not he knew it, and whatever he might be, Robin whose true name was Halacre lay now under a huge and heavy curse that surely would never be lifted but would follow him far beyond the world into eternity.

The moving trail of light came down from the higher forest to the beginning of the village, that straggled narrowly towards the church. Now coming so near the end of the journey the curious murmur of conversation ceased and all went silently. Doors opened along this road, and there came more, both women and men, to join the rest. The nearer to the church, the larger grew the crowd, and now the sound was of feet along the soft roadway, and the rumble of the waggon's iron-bound wheels, with the steady rhythm of Iris's hoofs, the lighter tread of the pony, that went unshod.

At last they came to the church and paused by the gate, where long ago in the priest's room above, Piers's father had shared lessons with the sons of Lewis Mallory. Ursula and Lilias dismounted, and waited till the coffin was firm on the shoulders of Morphew and Hendall, Awcock and Ade. Then Ursula took her mother by the hand and followed after, the

Jollands, father and son, close behind.

The new priest waited at the porch, and looked nervously towards the coffin, as if to find more pagan offerings, but it was bare. Even so, Ursula feared for a second that he might plan to conduct the whole ceremony at the porch or the graveside – and if so she might have been ready to fight a way in. But although not welcoming, he turned and proceeded up the nave. This church had seen Mallorys and Medleys baptized and wed and buried over many long years. Though all others lay in the graveyard, Master Lewis Mallory and his wife, Dame Cecily, who had been a Jolland, stayed side by side in the big tomb with its flat top that stood a little to the right of the chancel. It was by instinct, not instruction, that the bearers set down Piers Medley's coffin on the tomb of his grandparents and stood back.

The order of service then was austere and not too long. The passing bell made the only music, but the still flaming torches lit the place and gave it the magnificence that earlier custom would have provided but that rigidity beyond any known yet in these parts most sternly denied. The paintings adorning the walls were faded now, in many cases defaced, for the place had known some brief extremes in King Henry's reign. The pale colours, the lines of figures barely seen could still tell a tale to those whose grandparents had known them better. Here were saints without faces, angels without feet, wingless cherubim; a prophet's great beard, St Jerome's lion, the scallop shell of St James; Elijah's pointing finger and the sandals of Christ. The weather, penetrating the porous stone of the walls, had painted other pictures, where great patches of green mould turned with ease into far pastures, high hills, distant mountains of hope and promise . . .

The torchlight shone on all this and set beneath the

high wooden vaulting of the roof a great glow of consolation. Not that Piers Medley had been great but simply that he had lived and been known. Not loved, perhaps, as gently as his brother Richard had been loved; sometimes lacking strength but never understanding, always with time to listen, whatever the tale might be – either to laugh when he heard it and encourage the teller to better sense, or to set about righting some real or imagined wrong.

As the coffin was lifted once again and carried out into the air, it was recalled that this had been Master Medley's favourite son.

Very soon, all was done. The horses were waiting and Sir Francis lifted Ursula into the saddle, then turned to help her mother.

They returned the way they had come; this time in silence and with torches quenched.

11

No Going Back

Almost with relief, Ursula and Jolland watched his father ride away three days later. Both wanted only to guard him from learning of Humfrey's presence about the forest, hoping that by the time he came again some magic would have removed the threat. And Sir Francis might well return before long. He had undertaken to set agents about the task of seeking out Harry Medley or his sons, and would himself bring any news there might be.

Speaking of Piers's last instructions, Ursula had longed to tell not only why Harry or his son must be found and a small shabby book of Latin poems be given into his hand. But she had sworn herself to silence and could not speak the secret name. During this brief visit, she had had no word alone with Francis, for Lilias remained at Mantlemass and seemed unable to leave her daughter's side.

But although Ursula waved Sir Francis on his way with a lonely heart, she rejoiced, as Jolland did, that he had learnt nothing of his eldest son.

'And when he come next, we must pray your brother shall be fled.'

'Best he never knows my brother still lives. His mourning's long done – and now he has two more sons to take the place of Humfrey – and of me.'

Neither was willing to speak aloud what might happen before Humfrey Jolland left the forest, or how any disaster should be averted. If he had come, he had come with a purpose; if he went away without its accomplishment, then he might well return. Nothing was resolved by the fact that Jolland had gone twice in the last days to spy on the cottage and had seen no sign of life. It was folly to suppose the business should be easily mended, but both Ursula and Jolland needed comfort and were ready to cheat themselves.

'What might Peter know?' Jolland wondered. 'You said he'd be our man for sure come we need him.'

'Not yet,' said Ursula. And again she set about deceiving herself. 'Maybe their master has called them home. Maybe they are safe gone … Maybe it was naun so bad as we thought … Maybe there's just some man looks like your brother – his double, as they say, and come here for no more'n a bit of safe hiding …'

He did not bother to reply. They both knew that only 'maybe their master has called them home' made any sense at all.

'Ride to Plashets now, cousin. Work has to be set going again. None can mourn too long.'

Pilgrim had recovered, so Dick Ade saddled up and soon Jolland rode on his way.

Ursula went indoors. For the first time for days Lilias was nowhere to be found.

'Agnes – what come to my mother? Is she gone from Mantlemass?'

'She rid out on Folly, madam – some little time past. She told Joan Ade she'd matters to see done at Strives.

Joan thought she meant to bide there a little time, and then return.'

Ursula saw clearly that before Lilias kept her promise to settle at Mantlemass, she must look to this and that about her own home. All the same, she was uneasy.

'I wish she'd not gone.'

'She made no worry of returning.'

'I would she'd stayed a little,' Ursula insisted.

She though of Lilias returning to influences that had already harmed her greatly. She thought how Nance's son had been employed – if not paid – by the men dwelling secretly in the forest.

'I doubt Nance Tester, Agnes. All these years and I never thought to do so. Now I wonder – does she urge my mother on with her draughts and her potions?'

'If so, it'll not be much longer.'

'Come wi' me to Strives. Let's go now.'

The weather was overcast, and that stillness that comes with early spring, a sudden lessening and easing and shifting towards fullness, was laid over the forest like a spell. There was a scent of growing, the rich sweetness of golden broom bursting into flower after staying a long time tight and secret. Broom – *planta genista* – emblem of the Plantagenets, once Kings of England ... There was a sprig of the flower pressed and preserved and set carefully among those papers that went with the secret book.

Ursula paused to pluck a sprig of broom, then thrust it in the fastening of her dress ...

It was a pleasant walk from Mantlemass to Strives Minnis, the track beaten and widened by many years of coming and going between the households though threatened now with briars. The two women walked easily and slowly, as always in sympathy, speaking a little of Master Piers, not yet attuned or even fully aware of their loss; as if, the first loss swallowed, death keeps the senses quiet a little before the truth strikes home.

As they came near Strives there was smoke rising, and when they reached the place, they saw Lilias sitting leisurely on the bench against the wall, watching the activities of Nance Tester.

Her face red, her sleeves rolled almost to the armpits, Nance was staggering from the house with a great basketful of goods, which she then tossed on to the fire, fiercely burning in front of the house, and clearly already fed by such other loads.

'Nance is setting the place to rights,' Lilias said. 'If I'm to leave, I'll leave all spick and sprugged.'

Ursula did not ask what Nance was burning, for the contents of the basket, and soon of another, and another, fell into the flames with a tinkling and a clattering, and soon there were explosions, phials expanding and bursting apart as the heat took them. Then the fire soared blue and green, yellow smoke gushed and billowed, smelling of incense, then changing to a stifling fume, so that they all started coughing.

'There's to be naun left, daughter, depend on that. Nor I'll never set to brewing or distilling from this day. I did misuse that gift and God punished me sore for my weakness. Now, see you, I made that weakness a strength.'

There must have been shelf after shelf, cupboard after cupboard full of bottles and flasks, of porcelain jars and boxes, of dried herbs, barks and fungi of all kinds. Then Peter came shambling in, carrying a spade, and set about the herb beds as Lilias directed him, tearing out old growths, battering new, until nothing remained of rue and agrimony and hemlock, of thyme and feverfew and hyssop, of spurge and coriander and of mint.

Within the compass of little more than an hour, all

evidence of Lilias's skill in these matters, learnt as a girl from her mother, encouraged and enlarged by those years she had spent before her marriage in a great household, was totally destroyed.

The last basketful went into the fire. It was of crystals that turned all to flaring, spitting light, then utterly dowsed every flame and every spark leaving only blackness and ashes.

Lilias then rose from the bench and straightened her shoulders.

'Best done,' she said. 'I'll be indoors now and load what things I need. Folly must play packman. Bide easy till I'm back.'

Ursula and Agnes did as they were bid, sitting side by side on the bench that had stood against the wall of the house ever since Ursula could remember.

'Who shall dwell now at Strives?' asked Agnes.

'Best forestall a grievance – Nance shall have it. Howso she seem to me now, she served my mother long – and well enough in the old days.'

So then for a while they were silent, hearing Lilias moving in the house, talking to Nance – then her voice gradually rising, as if she looked for what she could not find and impatience overtook her.

Ursula looked at Agnes and smiled, then rose and went indoors.

Lilias's belongings were tied in two bundles, but she had also the great book in which all the business of Strives Minnis was set out – the men employed, the loads of ore carried, the iron produced, the wages paid. Something to do with this book was causing Lilias to shout at Nance.

'Who move it, then? Who touch it? I said never to shift it – you know that.'

'The place need to be cleaned! Fine high words there'd

be, come I left the dirt and the dust and the smoke and the gubber.'

'There were papers loose – three papers . . . What come to 'em? You never threw 'em away?'

'They'd've fell out and got trampled, and then I'd for sure've taken 'em up and put 'em on the fire. What else'd a tidy soul think to do?'

'What's lacking, mother?' Ursula asked.

'Drawings Dan Morphew made once – years ago, years. Plans for forging and such. Kept for his sake, for memory. Much I owed him. More a friend than a servant.'

She looked vengefully at Nance.

'And why'n't you drawn the fire. I'll have that fireback – send it after, soon's it cools. Timothy Morphew done that when he's still a lad. See it reach me by two days. It carry my emblem – the lily's on it . . . Now – bring out the bundles. My daughter's not to stay waiting while you doddle about your work.'

Nance snatched up both bundles, grumbling and muttering, shooting glances of near hatred at Lilias. But as she went to the door her tone changed and she began to cry loudly, gulping and sniffing.

'A fine end! A fine end!' she cried.

'Let be, mother,' Ursula could not help laughing at the fury and the frenzy and the sudden tears. 'Sad you lost Dan's work, surelye. But how long, in truth, since you set down to look at it?'

'Long enough, maybe.'

'Folly's loaded. Time to go,' called Agnes from the gate.

As the three of them and the pony headed along the track to Mantlemass, Lilias did not once look back at Strives Minnis, where for long years she had been Master.

At noon, Jolland returned from Plashets and sat down to

dinner with the rest. He had had no chance of a word with Ursula, for he came late to table. He was absent in manner, as she saw at once, but whatever he wished to say to her must wait. There was too much strange knowledge between them that could not be spoken here. Besides, the mood about the table lent itself to silence – it was the first meal at this board of the household on its own since its master went to his grave.

Once the meal was done with, Ursula was able to take Jolland on one side.

'What of Plashets? Was much lost through drawing the fires?'

'Less than could've been ... Cousin – Watkyn is there yet. So they are not gone. It is all still to come.'

His anxiety touched up hers. 'They went – and returned ... It must be soon they do what they come for – whatso that be. Shall you go again by Halacres, Jolland? And if your brother's there – should you – should you speak wi' him?'

He did not answer. He was pale and she knew and understood his fears. For at any time now, action must be taken, and whatever it should be it could only harm his brother, maybe bring about his death. Ursula did not greatly care what happened to Humfrey Jolland, but his father and brother she would protect with all her might. If justice were called upon and the strangers hauled away to the town gaol, then Humfrey would be tried as a traitor, condemned as a traitor and all his family would be disgraced. It was all so desperate and dangerous that Ursula found herself once more trying to comfort herself and Jolland with foolish suppositions – that these men were no worse than poachers, that they would soon be gone, that they might well have no knowledge, even, of Robin and the Ghylls Hatch horses ...

'And so they live in his old home? And have Peter Tester to bring food? And treat him so? And be so easy about the place? And with Watkyn one of the number – that got himself made a worker at Plashets?'

'Well – come it's so – the worst that we feared ... Then you must speak to your brother.'

He turned away in silence, and later she watched him leave Mantlemass and set out on foot. Only after he was gone there came a recollection and a sudden startling doubt. She went at once to look for her mother and found her with Agnes and the children in the little parlour. Lilias was always stern when she considered it fitting and had said always that children should not be indulged. But her grandchildren had set her on a different course; having her here at home, Ursula thought, would almost certainly be Susan's ruin and she had sooner her mother indulged the delicate Lewis, lest he have shorter time to be made happy.

The children ran to Ursula as she entered, but left her quickly to return to their grandmother, delighting in the novel idea that now she would live all the time at Mantlemass, and share their home, and be ever on hand to pet and cosset them and feed them sweetmeats.

Ursula sat down with them, pulling Susan on to her knee and teasing her for struggling.

'Have you forgot your own mother, since you have one grander. Go to her then, and I will have Thomas only for my boy. Look how he hold out his arms, the mommet. Thomas love me still and I shall love Thomas best of all!'

Susan only wriggled away, and ran again to Lilias; she was a child who would always know how best to get her own way.

'Agnes tell me I shall have the great chamber that was Master Piers's,' Lilias said. 'Is it so?'

'He'd wish it. But there's the little room next mine,

should you think better.' She smiled, for she was comforted by having snatched Lilias at last to live more easily. 'It's fully small.'

'I slept all these years in a room little bigger'n a bed – and once you shared it. But let it be as you think. When God wills, I'll die where my – where Master Piers died.'

Ursula now said what she had come to say, but found difficult since she greatly feared what she would learn.

'The papers you mislaid, mother – Dan Morphew's work that was in the Strives book . . . were the drawings of delicate things, like sconces or fine lanterns?'

'Fine enough,' said Lilias, with her short laugh. 'Guns, daughter. They were patterns, as you might say, of guns. You should remember. You wrote out the measures of 'em yourself, though that were long ago. There was the new boring that Dan only forged but twice. Have you forgot?'

When Jolland reached Plashets, having taken the long way by the cottage, he was tired from going on foot and much disturbed in mind. At first he had seen no one, but smoke was rising from the chimney. In despair at knowing so little and fearing so much, he had crept up to the cottage and peered through the window. There was a man sitting at the table, arms folded, his legs stuck out straight ahead of him, his eyes closed, his mouth open. It was not Humfrey, nor Watkyn, who should in any case be at Plashets at this hour; nor was it Robin Medley. It was a fourth man who sat there, another stranger. Yet not so strange, as Jolland saw when the man stirred, closed his mouth, and sitting upright ran his hands through his sandy hair and smoothed his sandy beard. The glass in the window was greenish and flawed, but even though this distorted the man's features, Jolland knew him because he knew so many of his family about the forest. His name would be Henty, one of a numerous tribe, loyal and devoted all save one – and he was the one who had been turned off by Master Richard. Jolland had heard the tale often enough, and now he remembered it in every small detail. Richard Medley had realized almost at once the mistake made in sending the man away – it had nagged at his conscience and his common sense ever after until he died . . .

Jolland had stayed there at the window, staring at Henty, knowing what he risked but unable to drag himself away, and marvelling at the malice and ingenuity that could so seek out and link together men of the same treacherous mind.

When at last he reached Plashets, Timothy Morphew was looking out for him and came at once to speak with him, drawing him a little on one side.

'There's that should be told you, Mus' Jolland. Let it, if you please, be now.'

The furnaceman's solemn manner told Jolland what sort the matter must be, and so it was; only in worse proportion than he was prepared for.

'You said to look to the gunstore,' Timothy said. 'So I did – and all was sound. Only, because of your words, I went again, this very mid-morning, to cast an eye over the ordnance. There's one small cannon bin carried away.'

'How could that be?' Jolland spoke almost absently, his mind racing over what must come now of horror. 'No easy load, Timothy. And when should it be – the pit being in sight by day and in sound by night – so near to your own housing.'

'There was a night you forgot, master. When none stay in the place save an old woman or two. The night we bury Master Piers.'

The shock of this silenced Jolland as surely as if

Timothy had dealt him a great blow over the head. He could say nothing, staring and fumbling for words and finding none. Now for certain there could be no going back. The worst was upon them – and it was for him to act.

'A small cannon? What sort of small cannon?'

'One o' them my father made – that was never in use. It waited, so he tell, till its day come. But that day never come for him or for his gun. A pretty sort o' thing, that cannon – someways a falconet, some ways a serpentine.'

'But heavy, for all that.'

'Four hundred pound, maybe – but to carry pound shot, like a falconet.'

'How could they have hauled it off so easy? Do you see signs?'

'This ground's much trampled, day b' day – and more so since the crowd that follow Master Piers to Staglye. When that crowd come home, there was a fire built for'm, and his memory drunk, and prayers for his dear soul's safety ... If the gun took out that same night – then its traces got shifted and there's naun seen of it.'

This might indeed be so, for they would have used slings to lift the gun, which was slender but smallish, and the men who had done so were none of them weaklings.

Yet there was more that plucked and tugged at Jolland's troubled mind. What good, he asked Timothy Morphew, should one gun be? It was a strange design – how would they know the way to make others like it, without calculations that would give the exact composition of the metal? Or if they were skilled enough – and both Henty and Watkyn were ironworkers – why had they not by now taken the cannon clean away – and gone with it? But he knew that two at least remained – again Henty and Watkyn.

'Truly it were a new and secret firing,' Timothy said, frowning. 'My father tell me that. It could be there's no other man, be he never so set-up, as'd make what my father make.'

'Then perhaps – when they raised it and looked close – they saw just that – they did know their ignorance and hid it . . . If so, there's little to grieve.'

He appeared almost painfully hopeful, so much so that Timothy frowned, looking already doubtful and astonished. This was a poor showing from the young man he had admired.

'Come it were hid near, then I'd find it. At best, Mus' Jolland, there's one weapon in the ugly hands of an enemy – who knows but the King of Spain himself. But at worst . . .' He broke off, shaking his head.

'At worst? At worst – what?'

'Did I not tell, sir, how the Widow Godman had her daughter come to Strives, and how she writ down the matter of the ore, and how much and how long to fire; and how much of an alloy, and how to bind it . . . Do you recall?'

He did, and with mounting despair.

'You mean, I see, that if such matter might reach the hands of – of a traitor – and spy . . .' Now he thought of Peter Tester, and his comings and goings between Strives and the cottage. 'Who holds such matter now? Is it the Widow Godman?'

'Who beside? And if, as told, she goo now to dwell at Mantlemass, then best she know what's afoot and take all wi' her to safety.'

'And no delay. Aye – it shall be seen to, and quickly.' He hesitated a moment. 'Is there any you suspect here at Plashets?'

'The man Watkyn. Who else?'

'No other?'

'No other from Plashets need be thought on. I praise God for it. But, I tell you, master, Watkyn work wi' others, whoso they be. I set to follow him to his lodging. And that lie strangely deep. Halacres had it – that was weavers and then got better set up. Tumbled many year; now built up. There lodge our Watkyn and one other I know from time past. One o' the Hentys, him that swore to bring harm to Master Richard, God rest him. And there was another besides – one I'd no way to name – though I do bluv I see'm one time about the forest – and that not long since. He wear a russet cap. If I'd seen a fourth, I'd not have wondered. For Halacres come the property o' that Robin Medley that took the horses and killed Master Piers by it, and none know where he rest now – but I'd hope 'tis deep.'

Timothy had talked longer than Jolland or any other had heard him, and now he only added,

'There's all my thought fo' you, master. Do you say, now, what's next to be done.'

12

Quarry

Straightening his shoulders and endeavouring to look purposeful, Jolland said firmly that he would consider how to act. Before an hour, he seemed to suggest, he would have acted, and for the best.

Trying to regain some dignity in the face of the man's plainly seen doubts, he strode off smartly and purposefully. Timothy would have expected him to call the men round to him, to sieze Watkyn and to threaten him. It made him queasy to consider the many ways by which a man in these surroundings could be made to talk. But for Jolland the time had not, in any case, arrived when Watkyn should be challenged. The strange and tenuous ties of blood and kinship remained to plague him. This was his brother, whom he had not greatly loved. Yet he must for his father's sake at least attempt to save Humfrey, traitor or no. Ursula had said that Plashets men would kill any traitor, and he knew she was right. If they killed him, though he was Master, who should blame them?

He went fast along the wide track – and met Ursula riding to find him with news that made him groan.

'Timothy Morphew spoke of this, cousin. Now, God

save all, they've a gun for model and the process for more.'

'Then – what next?'

'I'm bound for Halacres,' he said steadily. 'Best you return to Mantlemass. For what come next I dare not wholly think.'

'Can you not *see* what come next?'

'You know well – that eye's blind that used to show such matters,' he said, purposely misunderstanding her. Nor did he need that eye to show him.

'We cannot stay silent now!' Ursula cried.

Without answering her, he went on his way, nor did he turn to see if she indeed wheeled back to Mantlemass. He went on doggedly, with that swinging pace that disguised his limp; he could not afford to acknowledge any weakness, whether of his mind or his body. If he hesitated he would never force himself on again, for his dread of challenging his brother chilled and terrified him.

As he came within sight of Halacres, he saw at once that the door was open, and that a man stood on the step. He was leaning there with his arms folded, as if waiting. His manner, easy and unthreatened, his good clothes, his decent boots, aroused in Jolland a strange confusion of emotions. There was something rough and hard about him, the stamp no doubt of a man living on his wits, yet his still graceful posture took Jolland's mind back to the days when his brother cared most of all to be known as a gentleman's son. For all his apparent ease and confidence now, some suspicion or doubt must, since Jolland last saw him, have given him cause for concern. He had shaved off his beard and his hair was only half as long as it had been. These changes, undertaken as they must be by way of disguise, removed the last thin doubt that Jolland could have been mistaken and that this was no more than a 'double' of his brother. Without the beard the face, though so firmed and tautened, was still the face of that self-opinionated older brother, whose scornful teasing Jolland remembered too well.

Now the moment was approaching, he felt calm. Expecting no way out of the ordeal he went towards it with sudden confidence; and not the confidence that can come of despair, but a strong determination. Also some spurt of anger was moving in him. It was intolerable that he should be so placed – that he must jeopardize all he cared for in an attempt to retrieve the family honour that Humfrey had already thrown away.

With no lessening of his pace, he walked on towards Halacres, waiting for the moment when Humfrey would look up, see him and break off the almost soundless whistling that gave him an air of such ease. As it chanced, Humfrey's attention was caught by something indoors and he turned and went inside without seeing Jolland.

For the first time, a small gulp of pure fear took Jolland in the throat. He had senselessly counted on his brother being alone, though it was no more than an hour or so since he had seen Henty at the cottage. If there were more than one, how might the matter go?

Not daring to hesitate, he strode on, came to the door, shoved it and went inside.

Humfrey's back was turned. The pot hanging above the fire had boiled over and the flames were hissing about soup or stew. The movement at the door brought him swinging round, his hand already on the knife he wore in his belt.

'No need,' said Jolland. 'We are brothers.'

Humfrey paused. Then he said cautiously,

'What do you bring?'

There was a strange overlay to the words, as though his tongue would be happier with other syllables. Jolland saw that his words had been badly chosen, suggesting some secret brotherhood, rather than that of blood – a brotherhood in which key words and passwords would be used, and phrases left unended to be concluded by the newcomer.

'You mistake me, Humfrey Jolland. I am your brother. I am Roger Jolland.'

Humfrey stood for a second as silent as a stone, then he turned red in the face and shouted out, 'In the name of God, why are you here? Why do you come to this place? My brother? You? Why, you forest lout, what sort of Jolland are you?'

'A better than you.'

'There's no brother of mine dwells in these parts.'

'But I dwell here. And I am your brother. And you know it, for all your bluster-fluster. So let me ask – what do *you* in these parts, for this is not your place I bluv. Shall I name you *señor* Jolland?'

Humfrey frowned. He looked slowly over his brother, noting, wanting to reject – but then as he came to that tell-tale twist to the foot, obliged to accept. He said carefully, bitingly,

'Damn you to hell.' He kicked a stool across to Jolland and sat himself on its fellow.

Jolland sat down, and for a moment the tension eased. They looked at one another across the table and neither saw anything he liked. Humfrey saw a countrified lad, rough-clad, a bit tousled about the head, his speech no better than some kind of forest jargon; while Jolland saw a brother who appeared now many times more than the year or so between them. His speech, too, was tainted by an alien inflection, while his mind was treacherous, his intention vile. Jolland no longer expected to learn otherwise.

'My father believes you drowned.'

'Let him think so, then. I was picked from the sea by a Spanish boatswain. *Ero prisoniero* – I was a prisoner. You have never known imprisonment, my good brother, and eaten mouldy bread the weevils turned to crumb, and wept and sobbed for a drop of water, and felt your wrists and ankles rubbed raw by shackles. So – wait how you judge. Wait! A hero may endure, but God failed to make me a hero. It took me two years and more to buy my freedom with a promise – a promise of service. Do you suppose I am the only one?'

'Are you free, then?'

'To keep my word to my masters. I am free to do that.'

Jolland said urgently, leaning forward, wanting to put his hand on Humfrey's arm, but knowing better, his first purpose confused –

'Come with me now to Mantlemass! You need never go back. Bide in your own place! You're an Englishman, surelye!'

'Surelye!' mocked Humfrey.

Now it was Jolland who reddened, but he urged again.

'You'll not be found, here in the forest. Who's to know? Who shall hear of it once you get to Mantlemass? Later – go home to our father.'

'Never. That shall be never. Never. *Me han dado un en cargo y es mi destino* – I have a task to perform and that's my destiny. And I am not alone. We have a duty, each to the other, to save or destroy. Do you understand?'

'Watkyn – ?'

'Watkyn. He too has known captivity. And the third's a man a kinsman of ours turned off – a great injustice that burns in him still.'

'Yes – Henty. How do your – your masters – seek out such as Henty?'

'Men with a grievance will always drift together.'

'There's a fourth,' Jolland said steadily. 'Four of you in it. Where's Robin Medley, brother Humfrey?'

'Ah – Robin. He died, brother. *Perdóname.* Forgive me – that was no choice of mine. It was the horses we needed – not Robin Medley. The horses are where one day they shall be most useful. I cannot tell you how Robin Medley died – but he is gone, and his body lies under the sea. God rest him – *surelye*!'

'It's known there are spies about the forest,' Jolland said flatly, 'and two of them named. They're not easy men that work at Plashets. Best be on your way, for they'll be bound to come looking. They know the place you bide and they know the gun's gone from the pit. And I know, as do others that you've the plans to make more – was it Peter Tester brought that matter all writ down and tidy?' A sudden thought struck him. 'Or are you waiting on him now?'

'I'm waiting for dark, nothing more. Henty went this morning. Watkyn's to follow. We know where to meet.'

'I'll see you safe away – come you hand over the papers stolen from Widow Godman.'

For the first time, Humfrey looked sharply surprised.

'The bumpkin can bargain, then? To no avail, I fear. Henty has what you seek. And by now he's on the way to where the horses are kept.'

'You should fear to tell me!' Jolland cried.

Humfrey looked at him lazily, head to toe and back again.

'No,' he said. 'I see very little to fear.'

'Plashets men are dangerous men – I'll tell you again! The gun's moved – the furnaceman knows what was set down – it was his own father found the way of it. However it was learnt of – learnt it was. Though of all this I do see least why Peter Tester and his mother should betray Widow Godman.'

'Ah – then I see there are some things I know of this forest that not even you have learnt. Nance Tester is Henty's sister. The Henty's are many – you know that.'

'Who helped you to such matters? How should you know these things? No! Say naun of it! I see who it must be.'

'Robin Medley – who else? Was not old Goody Henty his nurse – and Will Henty her nephew? It chanced very happily that she set about some little revenge of her own. That was our benefit. There was none else left living, I'm told, who knew the truth of his father's death. No doubt she put her own gloss upon it – which served well. A year more and it could have been a different tale, for she died then.'

'You know too much. It make little sense.'

'It makes the best sense. Do you suppose that spies are sent only from England into Spain? That Spain keeps none in England? I promise they are many. And they are such as know well how to seek out the easiest consciences.'

Jolland stared at his brother, listening and understanding very well, yet at the same time deafened and blinded by the horrible simplicity of it. He had indeed been all this time a country lout, ignorant of true malice, ready to think the best. He had known, as Ursula had known, that Robin had been for years busy about secret concerns. But how should they ever have supposed him to be taking the way of those few from these parts who had become the bought men of a foreign power? If Robin was dead, then Jolland could only be glad of it – and he saw how many matters had worked his ruin. His uncertain situation at Mantlemass, his despair when he felt himself responsible for Humfrey's loss, those many years ago. It must have been then, scouring the ports and the coastal villages, that he first fell into the net. What it was that Goody Henty had added to all this, Jolland could not know – something, so Humfrey seemed to suggest, about his father's death . . .

'The gun,' he said, dragging himself back to the present necessity. 'Have they taken it, then? Watkyn – Henty . . .'

Humfrey laughed. 'A dainty little cannon, certainly – but hardly to be spirited away! It was hauled up for inspection, true enough – but you'll find it slid back into a hole not far from the pond. What need do we have of it – since all is calculated for us on paper? Do you think us fools? We travel light – not with cannon on our back!'

Jolland said, 'It's all but dusk. You did say you'd leave at dusk.'

'Aye, brother – so I shall. *No podemos retener el sol.*'

'What does that mean?'

'We cannot hold back the sun.'

It was now that Jolland came finally to his own weakness. He had called himself a man of iron, but the anxious spirit remained in him, the mesh of loyalties that tied his purposes, from which, now most of all, he could not find a way of cutting free. The thought of Humfrey being taken, of the truth of his kinship being revealed, with all that must mean, not only to his father but to those at Mantlemass, defeated him utterly. He knew he should deliver him up, and knew too that if he waited here long enough he would be looked for by Timothy Morphew; then matters would be taken from his hands.

He rose and went to the window, and stood there with head bowed, his shoulders hunched. Humfrey watched him, his manner idle enough, but his expression keen.

'Well?' he said, as Jolland stirred suddenly but did not turn from the window.

'If Plashets men find you they'll kill you, Humfrey Jolland. Make no doubt o' that. But you're my brother, God help me. I'll save you for my father's sake – naun else. How'll I ever see his face again, come I let you die?'

Humfrey shrugged and smiled. 'Your Plashets men, as you call them, need to be fleet to catch me. My plans are well laid.'

'Then get you ready to set 'em going,' Jolland said, still by the window. 'Plashets men are here.'

Ursula had turned Iris's head for home – then checked. She watched Jolland stride off along the track and soon he had vanished. His purposeful manner, his sturdiness and haste had touched her. But she feared for him, all the same. He carried no weapon but a small dagger that Master Piers had once given him as if to encourage his manhood. It was an almost dainty thing, in a fine sheath, and with the letter *P* engraved on the hilt. She cried out in amazement as she remembered this. She had first seen the dagger when she was still not much more than a child, and therefore had childishly interpreted the letter as standing for *Piers*. Now she saw that it must stand for *Plantagenet*. One day, she told herself, she would beg it back from Jolland, and put it with other things she might decide to include, in the small chest that was for the future to find – her granddaughter, who would have discovered the key . . .

As if this thought gave her new purpose, she then turned in her tracks and rode to Plashets. She doubted Jolland's ability to destroy his own brother. The determination must be hers.

She rode in and called for Timothy Morphew.

The first thing Timothy did, when Ursula had told him what she now knew, was to shout for his burliest men and send them to fetch Watkyn. He was not to be found, however, and no one could recall seeing him leave, or even pause in his work. For all that, they came upon his leather apron thrown down, the tools he had been using scattered alongside.

'Naun, now, to keep'm,' Timothy said grimly. He frowned and then looked at Ursula. 'Since the master o'Plashets is not here, mistus – do you give what order seem right. All here'll do your bidding, niver doubt. They know your mother's daughter when they see'er.'

'Master Jolland set out for Halacres,' Ursula said. 'You know where that stand? So be there's none but one there before'm, he'll do well. But ask me, it need but one other and these men being what they are – he'll be found in some danger. So I say, muster your men, Timothy Morphew. Get after my cousin – and then let be how't will.'

Jolland moved quickly from the window, shoving back Humfrey, who had come to peer over his shoulder.

'What – am I not to measure my adversaries?'

He was still mocking, and Jolland would have been glad to strike him – but there seemed little time for small quarrels.

'At least tell me how they're armed, my good brother.'

'As men in these parts do ever arm themselves – wi' the tools o' their trade. Hammers – pincers – shovels – tongs – shingling irons ... They're not such simple weapons. Not in hands used to 'em.'

At least Humfrey seemed to keep calm and unflustered. He said thoughtfully, though urgently,

'Watkyn and Henty are on their way. They're set for the coast. I'll be making further west. We'll join where the horses are.' He found time to grin. 'One day soon they'll be waiting for a Spanish landing – see if I'm not speaking true!'

'Never mind the horses now . . .'

'You and I are alone, then. Shall you speak up for me to your Plashets men – or let them hammer the life out of me?'

'No. For their sake I'll not speak to favour you. But I'll act the fool and let you go – and regret it the days of my life, could be.' Jolland clenched his teeth together, knowing the danger and the folly of the only course he could see. 'How much d'you know of the forest?'

'Enough to come and go.'

'Come they hunt you through it you'll be lost before you start.'

'You'll let them hunt me, then? Is that what you call letting me go?'

'Wait – and listen. I do this for my father's sake, never yourn. Once you're away there's none to know your name – you're no better'n no worse'n Watkyn or Henty – and so they'll see it. Gi' me your cap – you take mine. It's known in these parts. Mantlemass masters wear red caps. I may be the country lout you name me – but I know my way through the forest better'n I know my own mind.'

'What happens next – when we've done our clowning and exchanged caps?'

'It's clowning or death. Choose.'

Fastidiously, Humfrey took the cap Jolland held out to him.

'I'll go by the window in the cove,' Jolland said – meaning the single pane let into the lean-to built on the back of the cottage.

'You'll never do that without being seen.'

'I need to be seen, brother Humfrey – but the time's got to be right. If I'm stopped and held too soon – then we're done for. Both of us, maybe. But I bluv I'll burst through and be away. Do you bar the door and wait a little. Then take your ways. The track that crosses this'll take you north to the old road. You're not like to be hindered. The pack, see you, shall be hard on my trail.'

As well, he thought, with a freak of humour, as well brother Humfrey shaved his beard . . .

The window in the roof of the cottage, that slanted over a store for wood and grain, was far too small for Jolland to wriggle through without breaking the pane and tearing away the struts that framed it. Had Humfrey been going that way – or when he went that way, for he had best not leave by the door – he would have to hack away some of the thatch; his shoulders were half as broad again as his brother's. Jolland eased himself through, let himself down the slide and landed on his feet, since the roof ended no more than half his own height from the ground. He paused a second, staring across the open patch between him and the trees. The ground was humped with tufts of sedge grass and thin green rushes just making their small fringed tufts of flower. It would be easy to trip over any such hump and fall flat, and thus defeat the whole plan before it was a quarter-fledged.

As he had hoped and prayed, the Plashets men were converging on the front of the cottage, where the door would either open or be opened by them with force. But so long as that door was securely barred, and Humfrey could be trusted for that, it was stout enough, set in its thick stone walls, to resist being broken except with axes. There was an axe alongside the pile of firewood, but long before that was discovered Jolland believed he would have succeeded in leading the hunt off and away from Halacres. He hesitated. If he went too soon he would not be seen escaping; if he went too casually he would be caught too soon. Master of Plashets he might be, but he would not care to face the rage of these men if they discovered, while their blood was still hot and high, that he had planned to cheat.

He paused, getting his breath – then ran. He was suddenly filled with fear that they might recognize his limp, and because of it doubled himself up and moved in strange leaps over the hummocks that made the ground hazardous enough without any further elaboration. He seemed to be crossing the ground for ever. There was no sound at all but his own heavy breathing. At this rate he would be exhausted before ever the hunt was on or, with complete irony, get away among the trees without even being seen.

He had got to the broken stone wall and was clambering over it before, at last, he heard a shout.

'There a'goo!'

Jolland began then to flee through the forest in good earnest, ramming Humfrey's cap down to his ears. The shouting grew more distant, Jolland moved so well, but the actual sound of pursuit, of men thudding over dry ground, crashing through undergrowth, grew at the same time much heavier. They were indeed after him as he had planned. He smiled briefly, then hurled himself on, fighting thorn and bramble, skirting huddles of new birch and blundering over the stools of oak and beech, cropped long ago to feed the furnaces and sprouting tufts of twig and of leaf. If he proceeded along this bank, Jolland knew he would come to open heathland. He needed to show himself, but briefly; he could never keep ahead in the open. Also, skirting the edge of the open ground, concealed among stripling trees, there were many pits left

from old mining; they filled with water at this time of year, when springs and river gushed after the winter, and to fall into one of them could mean death by drowning. Thinking of this, for the first time he wondered where he should go to ground, how long Humfrey needed to get away, what eventual destination was to be reached – and when it was reached, what then? His pursuers would never be far behind, unless tricked by his circling and turning back on his tracks. They, too, knew the forest; and better than he, since most had learnt it from their fathers and their grandfathers.

The ground was spread with blossom – primrose and the blazing purple of wild hyacinth. And over all, the broom blowing, bending as the weight of blossom increased. The broom was good cover when he needed to pause, as more and more he did, and once a springing branch whipped the cap from his head. He left it lying. If it was found there might be a shout of triumph behind him, for Timothy would remember that the man he had seen at Halacres wore a russet cap. Seconds afterwards, he crossed a well-worn track and saw the hunt at its far end, silhouetted on the clean evening sky which by now held light only to the west. He stood poised, waiting. Then he heard a great bellow and hurled himself forward along a deer run that led him easily enough underfoot, but confusingly, so that he began to lose his direction.

Within these glades the dusk had come. He need not expect to be seen so easily. The change in the light was all that told him how long or how little he had been hunted, as so it must be for fox or stag or hare. But the increasing shadow encouraged him. He must surely by now have given Humfrey time enough to get clear. As he thought this and looked about him, he saw that for the first time he had indeed lost his way. He had no idea at all where he stood, or where this path would lead him, and as he paused and leant against a birch tree's silver trunk, he realized that he had thrown off his Plashets men. The forest was quiet about him. His crashing had silenced the creatures moving about their own concerns. Time itself seemed to have taken a swifter flight, for even as he saw the dark coming down the whole night was suddenly accomplished. He peered upward through the branches and saw no glimpse of sky.

Without intending it, he sank down and rested among the roots of the trees. He had better have kept going, for exhaustion took him like a blow on the head, and he had to struggle to stay conscious. He lay where he was, breathing deeply, half sleeping, until the moon rose and showed him the night-time forest and gave him an idea of direction.

He pulled himself up. The rest had done him harm, not good. His limbs had stiffened and his muscles knotted, and for a moment he was afraid to put his weaker foot to the ground. He began moving back cautiously along the little track, since he was uncertain where it would lead him. Thus he came again to the broad track where last he had seen the hunt. Where were they now? He could not believe they would so tamely have given up the chase. He turned on to the track and began to trudge forward – then paused to listen. Maybe they had waited for the dark to end with the rising moon and now moved on again. But he heard nothing. He saw enough of the moon now to show him that he was moving in the general direction of Strives Minnis. He would sooner have reached Mantlemass, for now fatigue had weakened him and he began to fear greatly the retribution that could fall on him for what he had done. He had not only cheated them of their rightful quarry but had fooled them, and they would not take that kindly. He had been mad to suppose that he would easily get himself out of trouble. Had he been a true Medley he might perhaps have done as he saw fit and defied the consequences. But he was only Jolland, however warmly they might have welcomed him in the past, and as he recognized this his weariness turned to dread and to fear. How should so honest a man as Timothy Morphew ever forgive his treachery? He must be seen as little better than his traitor brother.

Now surely there was a sound behind him. He looked back over his shoulder. There was a line of torches across the track and moving forward. They were distant, pin-pricks of light, but they came on steadily.

So once more he began to run. But only a sense of unreality had kept him going so long. The stride he had learnt so doggedly did little for him now. The pain in his foot and ankle made him cry out, and once he fell and almost rolled down a bank.

As he stumbled up again, he saw where he was. The bank ran beside the little river that emerged from a stand of coppiced birch and then flowed alongside Strives, whose pond it had once fed.

He turned along its course with relief, and as he did so he saw the second line of torches far ahead.

13

The Swans

From Plashets Ursula rode back to Mantlemass. She called out Dick Ade and those younger men who worked about the place.

'The King o' Spain sent a spy to the forest – set on to steal Plashet's guns and learn the way o' them. Go seek Timothy Morphew and say I sent you. It's like the spy may be lost about the forest. The more to hunt, the less he's like to get away!'

'He' she said; as if there were only one. But again in her mind's eye she saw four of them – Watkyn, Henty; Jolland's brother; her own husband. But now the tie meant nothing to her. All the years of her life, her father an iron man, her mother taking the task from him when he died, she had known the god-like quality of the metal, mysteriously burnt from the ground, and forged and hammered into the shapes men chose for it. The worst betrayal in these parts was the betrayal of iron – if she had never known it before she would have known it now, fiercely and possessively.

When the men had gone off as she ordered them, Ursula called for Agnes. She could not stay tamely at home, she said. Agnes begged her to consider and leave the men to the business. They argued loudly. At last Ursula flung away, shouting over her shoulder,

'Tell my mother where I'm bound. She'll not quarrel with me!'

She untethered Iris and mounted and was away.

She rode back first to Plashets and found the place deserted except for the women. Her own men had already come and gone. There was no one to consider that the dark must come down, and if the hunt was still on by then, then lights would be needed.

'Set torches ready for when they come back.' she ordered the women. Finding a poor supply, she stayed for a time helping to make new, blackening her hands and caring very little that she did so.

No one returned. The place stayed quiet. Though there might be clamour a mile or two miles away, here it was peaceful and still. A small child sat on the ground and threaded primroses into a chain, humming to herself as she did so. The dusk deepened and the child was called away. Ursula became increasingly anxious as the time went on and no news came. Where was Jolland now? Had he joined the hunt – if hunt there was – or were they all, hunters and hunted, gathered at Halacres, and had they caught their quarry and set about their own means of justice? Men had been hanged by their fellows before this. She saw the torches stacked, then once again got up on Iris and rode away. She turned the mare's head towards the track to Halacres. Once as she went she heard cries in the distance and once checked to listen. But the sound was not repeated, giving her no sense of its direction and making her wonder if she had heard no more than the crying of owls. But then, when she had urged Iris up that steep bank above the marshy ground she heard it again. This time there was no doubt, for it was the sound of any hunt, carrying within its deep note the terrible exhilaration of the chase.

Now the cottage was ahead of her. It stood quietly, unmolested. Then she saw a man shifting in the shadows, and called out.

'Who's that? Who are you? Leave skulking! Show me your face!'

The man shifted forward, stumbling a little, and for a moment she wondered coldly what she had called up. Then she saw it was Peter Tester. What part had he played in it all, she wondered angrily. But she spoke to him quietly, knowing she might need him.

'Where're your friends?' she asked; but her voice was sharper than she intended, because she was confused, now, and afraid for Jolland.

'They'll hang 'em!' he said; and began to cry. 'Hang me, too, will they, mistus?'

'What've you done that they'd hang you?'

'Naun but snared robbuts and such. Fed 'em else they'd starve. They said to pay me – but niver a coin seen yet.'

'Nor will be, now,' she assured him. 'They're spies and traitors and betrayed you, too – as certain as they betrayed the Queen of England!'

She dismounted and tethered Iris, who was growing fretful and tired.

'Come wi' me, Peter. I need to see inside this place.'

'The Queen of England?' he repeated, puzzling, his tears checked.

'Let be. Come, now – open the door.'

The door was firmly barred and resisted even Peter's unthinking weight, that hurled and battered till it seemed he must break his shoulders. Peering through the window, Ursula saw nothing in the gloom save the fire burned down to one small sullen eye. The idea was rooted in her mind that Jolland was somehow shut inside – left a prisoner, perhaps, while others escaped. Or maybe his own men from Plashets had found him there with his brother and turned on him as himself a traitor, and had done him some injury and left him lying.

The wildest of her thoughts seemed suitable enough, and the increasing dark offered no comfort.

'Peter?'

He had moved away. She felt too alone for endurance.

'Peter! *Peter*!'

The door opened ahead of her and she could just make out his face.

'Cove winder brusted,' he said.

'Then where's Mus' Jolland?' she cried. She shoved him back into the cottage. 'I must find him!'

'There's naun wi'in, mistus.'

She stirred the fire to give a bit of light, but it was almost burnt away. She went fumblingly through the place in the dark. But Peter was right. Dead or alive, there was no one there save the mice, and she went outside again, standing in the dark with her cheek pressed against Iris's neck, not knowing where to turn next.

'Best you get home,' she said to Peter at last.

He went off at once, and now she could see him, for the moon was up and its light growing. After he had gone she stayed in the silence, not bothering for how long, beginning, like Iris, to tire. She remembered how this had been Robin's childhood home. She tried to remember him as once he had been, but the image was lost.

At last she pulled herself once more into the saddle and began riding almost aimlessly, pausing at the head of every track to listen, hearing nothing, yet knowing the forest was not its peaceful self. There was more abroad than the night-time creatures, and it was as though all ears were strained, besides her own, hearing nothing yet knowing the unspoken sounds of danger.

Now in the moonlight, which had become veiled by thin scudding cloud that was being drawn up over the sky like a quilt, she saw that she had come near to Strives Minnis, and seconds later she was crossing the river by the pinnold and had come to the gate of the paddock where Folly had grazed for years. She slipped out of the saddle and hitched the reins over the gatepost.

Only then, as she turned, did she see the line of torches, not only ahead, but encircling and drawing in like a noose.

She spun on her heel and as she did so saw a man stumbling along the river bank and knew he was the quarry. He was on the point of falling to the ground, but what most filled her with horror and incomprehension was the way he moved.

She started towards him, and at the same instant Peter Tester came shambling down from the door of Strives Minnis. He held a flatter, a heavy hammer, in his right hand and was swinging it pleasurably as he came. It was a scene so like one she had witnessed once before, but long, long ago, that she almost fainted.

She shouted to Peter and ran forward, trying to measure the ground that lay between her and the fugitive, between the fugitive and Peter. She had a slight advantage, but Peter came down a sharper slope. She called out again and again, waving her arms as she ran. But he was wholly concentrated on his purpose and he had not the size of mind that would easily divide its attention.

'Peter! Let be! Wait, Peter! Wait! *Wait*!'

She reached him as he swung his arm, and flinging herself against him thought for a second that her own brains would be knocked out.

'It's Mus' Jolland, Peter! Can't you see it's Mus' Jolland!'

She heard the hammer drop. She ran to Jolland and crouched beside him as the torches closed in and the truth was seen.

Watkyn and Henty never got free of the forest, and no one would ask what happened to them; they would not be seen again, but what they had stolen was taken from them and returned to the Strives Minnis book of accounts.

But Humfrey Jolland had vanished clean away, and the shame and the fury this aroused at Plashets would be long in dissipating.

'They see me a traitor, too,' Jolland said bitterly. 'As how should they not?'

Ursula could not answer; she knew no way as yet of arguing round this matter. She knew the men stubborn, understanding and sympathizing with their mood.

For a week or more, Jolland stayed at Mantlemass exhausted and despairing and lame as never in his life before. It was well into the second week before he hauled himself up on Pilgrim and rode down to Plashets. Work was going ahead as usual, but there was no one about.

Then as he rode to the furnaceman's house, he saw Timothy Morphew walking back from the forge that was half a mile or so downstream. He approached without any hurry, and looked towards Jolland, but made no gesture of greeting. Jolland sat waiting for him, anxious, his hands hard and heavy on the bridle, so that Pilgrim tossed his head and shifted in protest. Timothy reached the open ground, around which the dwellings of the workers had been casually set down as they were needed over the years.

Without pausing, he continued over the green to his own house. He went inside, and pulled the door behind him.

The following morning, the furnaceman came to Mantlemass and asked to speak with Dame Ursula. When she came into the hall, where he had been left to wait, he greeted her respectfully and warmly; then he said – might he speak his mind?

'I should be glad to know it,' she replied. When he then hesitated, she said, 'Is it my cousin you'd speak of?'

'Aye, madam. I'm plagued to know what come to Plashets now.'

'What should?'

'We'm left wi'out a master,' Timothy said, looking at her under his brows, his one eye very anxious.

Ursula sighed. She knew it could only be so, for what Jolland had done had indeed been a betrayal, and save for the fact that he was now at Mantlemass, there was no saying what might have happened to him.

'I speak up too bold, maybe,' Timothy said, 'but there's naun to gain by shifty ways.'

'He had his reasons,' she said. 'That'll come hard to understand. Gi' me your hand to silence, like man to man, and I'll tell you the truth of it.'

Awkwardly but steadily, he held out his hand, and she put her own into it and pressed it, saying,

'Let there be trust between us. The traitor was his own brother, thought dead – all those years held in the enemy's country. For his father's sake – what else should my cousin have done?'

Timothy was silent, standing very still and thinking, and never taking his gaze from Ursula's.

'Aye,' he said at last. 'I do see it come hard. But he was thought dead – so what loss? Mus' Jolland saved his brother, surelye. But men do find that honour rank high in the world.'

She flushed at the rebuke, quiet as it was.

'Then shall he never be forgiven? Shall Plashets – that Master Richard Medley gave him – never see him master again?'

'One day. It could be. Aye – it could be. But not yet. The tale's raw in every mind. There's no man I know at Plashets could work for'm at this time.'

'So be it, then. But what of Plashets now?'

He hesitated a long time, and she knew no way to help him. She could not think what he wanted to say – perhaps that he should be master? She knew this would not do, for at the worst the men would throw off his authority, and at best they would mutter, thinking it unfitting.

'Madam,' he said finally, standing very upright, 'if I'm bold, then let you be merciful. There is a master of iron here at Mantlemass. Any man at Plashets'd take the Widow Godman for master – and be proud, as my own father was proud and taught me.'

Ursula smiled. For all Jolland's distress, this thought of Timothy Morphew's moved her so pleasingly that she felt renewed.

'Best you speak wi' her. She'll tell she's no longer young. If she come to be master at Plashets, as she was at Strives Minnis, and at Froreden when first my father died – it cannot be for many years more. But by that time she feel she must give up,' Ursula said slyly, 'shall my cousin Jolland be forgiven and take his place again?'

He was not to be blandished, but only said rather sternly that time was hard to measure and men's hearts harder still – yet both came to ends unseen.

'For sure,' she said. She smiled. 'I'll tell my mother you've come to speak wi' her.'

Past midsummer, well into July, a servant rode from Sir

Francis Jolland with word that he was coming himself to Mantlemass before the month ended.

Only that morning Ursula had paused to watch the swans fly over, and she felt that she had known he would be coming soon. She had not wept for the Robin her husband had become; but long and bitterly for the eager lad she had once known. Now in her heart she thanked him for freeing her. Though Francis remained securely wed, yet now she felt her own thoughts at least unfettered; they had dwelt on him ceaselessly since those days in the spring when her world had swung and shaken and altogether changed its complexion. Already it seemed long ago for her, the horrors had strangely eased away, losing themselves in wider necessities – the season changing, the business of farm and foundry, now brought close by her mother's changed way of living; the children growing, her comfortable reliance on Agnes's companionship; the fact of Mantlemass being her sole charge – at least until a true heir came to claim it, if he ever should. The sadness of Master Piers's loss, too, had already softened as time took its own way. Only Jolland's wretchedness remained like a canker that threatened and disturbed.

At first Ursula's whole care would have been to swear all to secrecy about Humfrey Jolland's return and what had followed. His father had long supposed him dead, and to revive hope only to dash it seemed cruelty beyond meaning. But there was too much besides – and how should any of them look him in the face and live out the lie?

So she had sat at her desk and written him a letter telling all the story, and despatched it sadly to him in London. Now he was coming himself in answer, and it would not be easy to see his renewed distress.

Sir Francis rode in at noon and they went straight to

table. The talk was of small matters, but he had embraced his son with a warmth so reassuring that Jolland began at once to revive in spirit. Later they sat talking together, and he said he had decided they should not speak much of what had occurred.

'We must have it ever in our hearts,' he told Jolland, 'that my son and your brother chose a traitor's course. Yet who shall say how you or I might have chosen in his place? We believe in our own strength and honour – but not all men are strong, and too many others know ways to make them weak ... Your weakness was to save him – mine, no doubt, to love you for it.' He sighed and shook his head. 'God wills all. Who knows his purpose?'

Then shrugging the matter away, he spoke of other things.

'A man I sent on the business of Master Medley's eldest son is returned. So I have news. That Harry Medley died some years past. The son who stands in his place is another Harry – though since his second name is John, for his mother's father, he was ever called Jack till his father died.'

'And did he prosper – did Harry Medley prosper?' Ursula asked.

'The Medleys of Dean Forest are of Ravenshall – that came to them from the family of Harry Medley's wife, Anne. They are well settled and of most honourable repute – so my man tells me.'

'That would please Master Piers,' Ursula said. 'I would he had known it to cheer him.'

'And now you know it, what shall you do with the knowledge?'

The secret seemed to her to hang between them. She longed to tell him what Piers had told her – the name, the royal kinship. But whatever else she might come to relinquish to him, loving him so dearly but so distantly over the years, yet she would be steadfast in this whatever it might cost her. Only if she ever had to lose Mantlemass need the tale be told, and then maybe only half.

'Master Piers left a book that had been his father's – that he said Harry should have. It was to mend an old quarrel he wished it – the quarrel that sent Harry Medley from Mantlemass. And now, it must be sent by some messenger to his son.'

'Shall I send my man that way again, then?' Francis asked. 'He is to be trusted.'

'I must think who best to send. But not a stranger.'

That night she stayed up a long time writing to Medley of Ravenshall. Into the front of the book she put a sprig of this spring's broom that she had been pressing. Also she carefully replaced that folded paper Piers had shown her, telling where a man had died and when ... *Anno Domini 1550 Rychard Plantagenet was buried* ... Then she sewed the book into a cloth cover and knew sadly that she must part with it. Though it held the power to bring unwanted change to her life, she could not believe that this would be so. And it was as if with young Jolland's seeing eye that she accepted a picture of herself living still in this place and dying here.

She went to bed at last, but slept little, thinking of too much, and knowing Francis not so far away. But just as dawn showed through the curtains, she saw suddenly who her messenger must be. Then she slept, and as soon as she went from her own chamber to begin her day, she set about finding him.

Only he was already coming in search of her.

'Best I should be the one to ride after Harry Medley,' Jolland said.

It would be a long journey. The summer was already far advanced, but the weather should carry any but the most faint-hearted traveller well into October. After that, there was no telling. It was unlikely that the traveller would be able to start for home before the following spring, for there were rivers to cross, unknown places to discover, and hazards, no doubt, to be faced.

'By next spring,' Jolland told Ursula, 'I shall hope Plashets men may think better of me. Now I am not let be Mus' Jolland I do understand how the iron come like a fever, and never let a man go.'

'So it is – and so my mother ever told me, and every other soul I ever knew who worked iron ... See you find new ways in Dean Forest, Jolland, and bring 'em to us here. And I'll pray daily that you'll be master again.'

Jolland set out from Mantlemass on the last day of July, and young Dick Ade went with him. This was the first time Jolland had been given a servant of his own and the fact replaced a little of his lost self-respect. He and Dick were much of an age, only Dick was forest-born. It would be a good partnership, not least because Ades had been about Mantlemass and Ghylls Hatch for generations.

'Miss me,' Ursula said, as she embraced Jolland. 'Remember I am some sort of mother to you – for so your own father said I should be.'

Jolland smiled over Ursula's head at his father, and promised, kissing her fondly, then turning away and catching Pilgrim's bridle. Dick jossed him up, and then with much self-importance mounted himself and rode sternly after his young master.

The household stood to watch them go, to wave and call blessings after them. The children jigged excitedly, and Thomas in Agnes's arms shouted as loudly as all the rest. Then the servants turned to go indoors, pretty Joan Ade in floods of scalding tears.

'Does she weep for her brother?' Lilias asked, preparing to make her own farewells and go to Plashets.

'She weeps for someone she loves, that's certain, madam,' Agnes answered her.

'I'll bide two-three days or so,' Lilias said to Ursula. 'There's much to do that maybe only I know how … Farewell, Sir Francis. Let it be soon that you come to us again.'

Ursula smiled. It was a long time since she had heard her mother's gentry voice, or indeed seen her so upright and commanding and strong – as she had been when she was master at Strives, before she had cause to cast away her physics and herbs.

It was a fine day, the sun high in a clear sky.

'Pray, Agnes,' Ursula said, 'see the children happy for I must attend our guest.'

'Aye, surelye,' said Agnes. 'But let me also see their mother happy.'

She paused a second to smile at Ursula, then went off with Thomas in her arms still, and Susan pulling Lewis after them.

Ursula and Francis walked before the house, leisurely and quiet in the sunshine.

'Shall we see our swans?' he asked.

'How should we? They are long gone. It must be evening before they come again.'

'Then shall I not return to London till tomorrow, madam?'

'You cannot return sir – so you wish to see our swans.'

'I do so wish … Only you must tell me that I am a welcome guest.'

'Stay,' she said. 'Stay …'

Soon the briskly moving riders had reached the head of the track, away from Mantlemass, away from Ghylls Hatch, from Plashets, from the forest they knew towards one full of the unknown, of mysteries. It was a wide, bright morning, and neither knew what adventures or what dangers lay ahead. It was the thought of this, perhaps, that silenced them – or else it was the parting.

'Your sister wept sore to see you go,' Jolland said at last.

'She bawled. Aye, she did. But not to see me goo!'

'What, then?'

Dick shrugged and shook his head, but slid a glance at his companion as he did so.

'Must a' bin to see someone goo, I'd suppose.'

There was a point between Mantlemass and the old road that crossed the forest north to south, where Plashets was faintly seen, the light catching the higher pond. A track from there led upward to the road – the track by which Humfrey Jolland would have travelled. There was a man standing at the crossing when Jolland and Dick Ade reached that summit.

'Timothy Morphew – come to bid you Godspeed, sir,' Dick said.

Jolland felt his spirits bound in hope. However arduous the journey, it could only be made lighter if Dick was right. Morphew would not likely come so far only to upbraid. Morphew it certainly was, and come of his own free will – then surely to wish the travellers well.

'Hold Pilgrim, Dick.'

Jolland dismounted and tossed the reins to his servant. He approached Timothy Morphew steadily but warily. The man for his part straightened up and lifted his chin and moved forward.

'I am glad to see you, Timothy. Do you indeed come to speed me on my way?'

'Aye.' He paused. 'And to wish a good return.'

Jolland could not answer this, for he felt that if he did he might throw his arms round Morphew's enormous shoulders and weep in sheer relief.

'It's a far journey, sir – here to Dean. More'n I'd care to travel. Not the fastest ride reaches journey's end. Watch you go steady. I seen a-many drop at the first trouble.'

'I am sorry, Timothy,' Jolland said in a low voice, trying not to look away from that blazing blue eye. 'Maybe I did see my duty wrong. Forgive me.'

'I've that of yourn must be returned. Hung on a tree, it were, halfways twixt here and there.'

His hand came round from behind him. He held out the red cap of felted wool that Humfrey had taken to wear as he made his way from the forest. Had he left it as thanks, or as an insolent snap of the fingers? Either way, that red cap stood for everything that Jolland feared he had lost for ever. When he wore it, he wore what Mantlemass men had, for some lost reason, worn as far back as Master Lewis Mallory. What Morphew was restoring to him was his acknowledged authority.

'Set it firm on your head next time you come to Plashets. I did think maybe that could be niver. But time goo over fast. My thought got changed a little even a'ready.'

Jolland held the red cap in both hands, warmly, as if he loved it. Then he held it out, still in his two hands, saying as he did so,

'Keep it for me. When I return – then, if you see fit, give it to me again.'

The furnaceman was not quite smiling, not quite frowning. His eye seemed brighter and more piercing than ever before. It challenged and encouraged – the challenge halfway to a threat, the encouragement nearly admonishing. But he took the cap again and stuck it in his belt.

'Goo your ways,' he said, turning at once to take his own way back to Plashets . . .

For all the rest of that day Jolland rode hard and merry, Dick at his heels and the future pulling them westward. They had food with them, and stayed at dusk to eat it close by a river whose name neither knew, and maybe never would know – it was only a place on the way. The water increased the sky's declining brilliance, and on the water many swans moved slow and graceful, then rose in twos or threes and flew upstream, their feet trailing a ruffled pattern on the surface.

'I hope my cousin Ursula shall think of me when she watches the swans fly over home. I'll think of her – and so make a sort of message. What d'you say, Dick?'

'Swans is only fowl, like any other, sir,' Dick said, contemptuous in a friendly way . . .

The same bright evening spread over Mantlemass, Ursula and Francis went to walk in the forest, and to scent the soft air, dusty with chaff from the early-cropped field alongside the farm. They walked side by side, speaking seldom, but it seemed to Ursula that their feet barely touched the summer ground.

'Shall we see them soon?' Francis asked.

'Yes. Soon. I am thinking of your son, and how I told him once – They mate for life; as we do.'

'Well, it is a known fact – it is truth.'

'Aye – it is true of the swans. . .' She held up her hand. 'There! Now! Listen!'

The sound of wings came from very far away, for the stillness was now entire. The high singing beat of the great wings made a music like no other. It came up from the south, where the river ran in from the sea and spread into

long valleyed marshes, and heron stayed for the last rising fish of twilight.

Ursula and Francis stood still and silent, gazing upward, following the glowing white of the birds against the sky, until the sound was swallowed. Then it seemed as if they two were all that remained of creation.

'Give me your hand,' he said. 'I shall take you home now . . . Shall we see them again in the morning?'

She hesitated for a second, but smiled, saying more to herself than to him,

'Let be how't will . . .'

The Mantlemass Novels

What happier fate for any author than to live in a setting that demands to be written about?

This good fortune came my way when I made my home, a good many years ago, in a part of Sussex where several thousand acres remain of that great forest that once spread over all this countryside. I had known the place since childhood but only for walks and picnics. Suddenly, there it all was outside my garden gate, viewed from every window, ancient, mysterious and challenging.

I thought all the time of what I would one day write about the place. Long before I knew their names my characters were moving secretly through the forest, daring me to begin their story.

It took me ten years to pluck up courage and make a start. 'Cecily,' I wrote, 'had been brought to Mantlemass at dusk . . .'

What I certainly did not realize as I paused to consider that first line was that the last line would not be written for another twelve years.

B.W.

The Lark and the Laurel – Wrenched from her idle and elegant life in London, Cecily Jolland is horrified to be left with her aunt in Mantlemass, deep in the Sussex forest. But unexpected freedom and her friendship with Lewis Mallory help Cecily grow into a spirited young woman, and she learns that life at Mantlemass has much to offer her.

The Sprig of Broom – For Medley Plashet, son of a humble forest guide, life is full of riddles. What is the significance of the sprig of broom? What dark secret shrouds his father's past? Knowing his future happiness to be at stake, Medley is forced to seek out the truth.

The Eldest Son – Harry Medley, hot-headed and arrogant, is as fiery as the iron furnaces he dreams of mastering. His passion for iron is only surpassed by his great love for his wife Anne. The Eldest Son is the story of Harry's maturing, of his frustration with his father's authority, and of how, through pain and sorrow, Harry comes to realize his ambitions.

A Cold Wind Blowing – Piers Medley's peaceful life is abruptly altered when his uncle is murdered, leaving in his care a strange and silent young girl with no memory, it seems, of her former life. Drawn to her against his will Piers is soon bewitched by Isabella. But despite the great happiness their love brings, Isabella's past haunts her still.

The Iron Lily – Orphaned at 15, strong-willed and proud, Lilias Rowan runs away to make her own fortune. When she becomes successful and respected she knows the time has come to seek out the Medleys of Mantlemass to discover the significance of the ring bearing the lark and laurel crest that her mother had left her.